To

Temporary
Permanence

Temporary Permanence

My Life In America:
Humorous Short Stories Based on Experiences Of a Japanese Engineer

Yashi Nozawa

This book is a work of fiction. Any resemblance to actual events or persons, living or dead, is entirely coincidental.

"Temporary Permanence," by Yashi Nozawa. ISBN 978-1-62137-050-5 (softcover), 978-1-62137-051-2 (eBook).

Published 2012 by Virtualbookworm.com Publishing Inc., P.O. Box 9949, College Station, TX 77842, US. ©2012, Yashi Nozawa. All rights reserved. No part of this publication may be reproduced, stored in a retrieval system, or transmitted in any form or by any means, electronic, mechanical, recording or otherwise, without the prior written permission of Yashi Nozawa.

Manufactured in the United States of America.

To My Mother

Table of Contents

Preface

Frank McCourt wrote his best-selling memoir, "Angela's Ashes" after he retired as a high school English teacher. When I retired at the age of sixty-five, I also decided to write my memoirs. I believed my life story to be as interesting as his, if not more so, especially my experience in pre-war Japan and my life during World War II. The project seemed to be insurmountable at first. I said to myself, hey, what else can I do after I retire? Retirement meant that I would be able to do anything I want. I had no definite ambition to accomplish. I didn't need to earn a living. Even without further increase of income I would be able to survive, even though my life cannot be called affluent in any sense.

I plunged into this project without further ado. At first I had to learn how to write in a presentable style. I wrote many technical or scholastic papers as an engineer, but they don't have the same style. I want to be readable by general readers, not fellow engineers and physicists.

I was intimidated by college writing courses because I didn't have as much humanities background as other students had. I couldn't afford the high tuition and major commitment of my time, either. I took several writing courses in adult education classes. A few courses were good, but most were a waste of my time for learning how to write. However, adult education courses were useful to help me realize that many people want to write, but few actually write something. Most had an excuse for not writing. They were too busy and had no time to write. On the one hand, some wannabe-writers had a good command of writing technique and language skill, but they didn't produce any writing. On the other hand, I, who lacked writing technique and had poor English language skills, did produce some. Naturally I got more praise than people who didn't produce any. The lesson I learned from these adult education courses is that I have to keep writing, despite my poor English and lack of experience. The more I write the better my writing will become. No excuses. Writing should be the top priority in my life. Then I will be able to write something.

So I started writing short stories based on my life experience. Whenever I had opportunities I attended local writers' meetings to obtain critiques on my short stories. I never attended high priced writers' workshops, which were often held in remote locations, partially due to cost, but mainly because instructors would reject my stories for poor English, not because of their contents. Eventually I built up confidence in my writing. When I moved to my present retirement community, I discovered that they had a monthly newsletter, Indianwood Arrow, a 16-page booklet. The publication welcomes any articles relevant to our community lives. This was my golden opportunity to present my life story in short articles. I sent an article every month. Fortunately readers' responses to my articles were favorable. At the end of the year 2001 I had already published a total of twelve articles. I assembled a booklet including all these articles plus three others which never were submitted to the newsletter and gave it as a Christmas present to my family and friends.

The last and most important remark is that all my articles, including this preface, have been reviewed and corrected by my beloved wife, Ann, for correctness of English language. Many people asked me how I managed

English so well as to write stories in my non-native language. The truth is that I never managed to learn English well. Even today, for instance, I have no idea when I should use the definite article "the" and when indefinite article "a." I often confused letters "r" and "l" because they are the same sound to my ear. These are a few of many defects in my English proficiency. I express my sincere appreciation for her effort and cooperation on my story writing enterprise and adventure.

Twelve months have passed since I assembled my short stories in a booklet titled, "From My Life." Meanwhile I wrote more stories for monthly community newsletters, "Indianwood Arrow" and others. My original plan was that making a booklet of my stories would be an annual event for a Christmas present for my family and friends. Due to a slight miscalculation in my part, I didn't make it in time the following year. I finally finished the project during my Christmas vacation. Christmas vacation for a retired person? Yes, I had Christmas vacation this year. I crammed up my schedule with many activities so that I couldn't find time to do actual work. Fortunately, most of my scheduled weekly activities such as computer coach in Blake library, writer's meetings in Port St. Lucie, and golf lessons at South Fork High took Christmas/New Year holiday recess also.

Many readers have asked me whether events depicted in my stories are true or not. My standard answer is that "the core idea of each story was based on my own experience." Naturally details and any reference to a specific name of person or company were fictitious to avoid liability. However, my advice is that readers should consider that all stories are fiction for your entertainment. In my opinion, each story should stand by itself for its value; the source of the story should not be in the way for readers.

Before I finished the second booklet, many things happened in my personal life and my writing career came to a dead stop. Meanwhile time passed quickly and I am facing now my 80th birthday. I decided on a final effort to put together all short stories and publish them in book form. This is the result of that effort and I hope many people will enjoy my stories.

March 2012   Yashi Nozawa

Part One
In Training

Today's Special

"Soup, please," I said.

"For breakfast?" the man behind the counter said.

I didn't know what Americans ate for breakfast. I wanted to order a typical Japanese breakfast of *miso* soup and steamed rice, but I knew they didn't eat rice. At least I could get a bowl of soup.

"Well, what kind of soup? There are all kinds." He pointed out the list on the wall. This would be my first meal in the U.S. I had just arrived the day before, but I hadn't found anything edible since then. I looked at the list but couldn't decipher what these names meant. Then I found it.

"Tomato, please." I had never had tomato soup, but I knew what a tomato was.

"Do you want toast with it?" he asked.

"Yes, please."

"What kind?"

"Yes," I couldn't understand what he was asking.

"White?" he seemed accustomed to ignorant foreign students. I was so hungry that I didn't care what he would serve. He placed two slices of bread into a toaster. Then he took a red can from the shelf, opened it, and poured its contents into a small pan on the stove.

"Soup from a can! Who could have such an idea? Only Americans could. America is fascinating," I thought. The idea might be good, but the soup tasted awful and the bread was too crumbly. My first breakfast in America was a disaster. I then realized that when I was in a strange country, I would have to endure any strange tasting food to prevent starvation or sickness.

I had arrived in the Unites States the day before, September 17, 1959. I had to change planes in New York on the way to Boston. It was the day Russian Premier Nikita Khrushchev visited the United Nations. Because of him, my plane was delayed. When I was finally settled into the YMCA in Cambridge, it was late afternoon. I hadn't eaten anything since the breakfast served on the New York plane. I immediately went out to find a suitable place for my supper.

To my surprise I couldn't find any eating-place there. I thought the YMCA was a cheap hotel, which I expected to have a low cost cafeteria. I ventured outside and started walking down the street. I walked probably 10 minutes but couldn't find any restaurants. I didn't want to go far and get lost. When I was ready to turn around, I discovered a busy store where people came out with bags of food. I could buy some food there, instead of finding a restaurant. I noticed the posted store hours. "We close at 6 pm." I checked my watch. Five minutes before 6. I rushed into the store and looked around. It was nothing like any store I knew. There were many shelves with stacks of various types of merchandise. But none was familiar to me. I was frantically running around to find familiar items with no cooking required. I found a section for bread and baked goods, but the shelves were almost empty. I grabbed the only remaining bag of bread, containing a full loaf. Bread was not a traditional Japanese food, but I had

had some before. In Japan you had only two choices in bread, half a loaf or a full loaf. When we ordered a half loaf, the baker cut off one edge of the loaf, halved it, and sliced it if asked to. A slice of bread was usually a half-inch thick. I preferred tearing a chunk of bread over a slice since I could feel its softness, moistness and stickiness.

Now I found bread, I had to find something I could eat with bread: jam, butter, ham, or cheese. I was worried about running out of time in the unfamiliar place. The lights dimmed. I found a can of ham. It seemed too big, a 3-pound can, but no smaller size was visible. I hastily went to the register and bought the two items. I was glad I managed to get food, even though it cost me almost 3 dollars. Considering the size of these packages, I would be able to have a minimum of ten meals from them. When I arrived at my scantily furnished room, I opened my package. I realized that I had no utensils, dishes, or can opener. Fortunately the tin can had a pull-tab. When I opened its top, I was shocked. Semi-transparent amber gel filled the can with a pink chunk of ham buried under the gel, instead of neatly sliced ham. I would have no way to eat this strange mess. I gave up on the ham. I had to be satisfied with bread alone. When I opened the bread bag, surprisingly it was already sliced thinly. However these slices bothered me. They were not white and had a strange smell. I bit into a slice. It tasted slightly sour. I spat out the piece. When I looked at the bag, it said rye bread. I had never heard the name. Whatever it was made of, it tasted as if it were spoiled. I gave up on the bread, too. My first night in the affluent country of the United States was a hungry night.

I was a penniless student, supported only by a governmental stipend of 5 dollars per day. The stipend had to cover everything except tuition, which was already prepaid. My plan was to spend no more than 3 dollars per day for lodging, only one dollar per day for meals and save the rest. At the end of the school year, I intended to travel and see the United States with the money saved. I had to watch every penny spent for meals, which was my only controllable expense.

My major concern during the first several weeks was finding a place for each meal, not the cost of the meal. Lunch was the easiest. I always went to the cafeteria in the Graduate House, which was open to all students. Many foreign students also favored that place. There were two lines during lunchtime, one for the steam table and the other for the grille. I had no idea what those names meant, but I always selected the line for the steam table. In the grill line, I had to place an order in a complicated way. At the steam table, I could simply point to the desired food with my index finger. It took me several months before I could go to the grille line and order a hamburger, medium, on a white roll, with lettuce and tomato. No, my comprehension of oral English didn't improve during those months, but I became acquainted with a few friends, and one of these friends told me how to order the hamburger. Even after such coaching, I still had trouble with ordering any other dishes in the grille line. I had no knowledge of available choices. Eating at the Graduate House was simple, but too expensive for me.

Meanwhile I rented a room in a private house, owned by Ms. Johnson, a sixty-ish single woman. The house had a total of two rooms to let. The other tenant was a man who worked at the Electric Company, according to Ms. Johnson. I never met him, but she seemed to prefer him to me, or she preferred a workingman to a student, especially a foreign one. She originally hesitated to rent the room to me, but the gentleman who accompanied me persuaded her. He was from her church. She was suspicious about my behavior. On the first day she gave me a warning that I should not use newspaper, or any paper other than bathroom tissue, in the toilet. She also added that no food was allowed in the room. My original plan to cook by myself and to save money evaporated in thin air. Fortunately, farther down the same street there was a supermarket, the First National. Every day on the way home I stopped there and looked for my breakfast, something I could eat without cooking. I found the ideal breakfast: a bunch of bananas, a loaf of raisin bread, and bottles of Coke. I ate this combination for breakfast every morning before I went to school. After the breakfast, I hid the remaining food in my suitcase and carried the garbage with me for disposal in the public trashcan on the street. I could not afford to take a chance, since Ms. Johnson occasionally came to my room for cleaning. I had solved the breakfast and lunch problems, but I still had trouble with dinner.

I walked to school every day. Along the way, I peeked into every store and identified several eating-places, greasy spoons. I tested all of them for their price and friendliness. I selected a small restaurant, called Joe's. Its prices were reasonable and the place was usually not crowded. Best of all, they seemed unconcerned about me. My next problem was what to eat. I was already accustomed to eating strange dishes with unidentifiable ingredients, but I couldn't match their names with the actual foodstuffs. One day I discovered an ingenious solution: "Today's Special." There I could get a different dish almost every day by ordering Today's Special. Since I had no preference for any specific dish, it was ideally suited for me. This scheme allowed me to learn a new dish every day while eating the lowest priced selection. The biggest advantage of ordering "Today's Special" was eliminating ambiguity in my pronunciation. It was humiliating when I ordered something repeatedly and the cook couldn't understand it.

In the beginning, I had no idea what I would get when I placed the order. Gradually I learned what a particular name meant by comparing the name with what I got, for instance Salisbury steak, fried chicken, drum sticks, turkey breast, pork and beans, spaghetti and meat balls, fish and chips, etc. I could order these dishes even in other restaurants, except turkey. I never mastered the pronunciation of "turkey" so that a short order cook could understand me. Anyway, my worry about meals was finally over, I thought.

One day I went to Joe's for late lunch rather than the usual dinner, since I missed my lunch hour at the Graduate house. I was the only customer, probably due to it's being the off-hour. It was just at the end of the busy lunch hour and too early for the dinner hour. I saw on the menu "chicken chow mein" as today's special. I never heard the name before. I had no idea what "chicken chow mein" was, so I was secretly excited at the prospect of finding out.

"Today's Special, please," I said.

"It takes a minute, so have a seat," the familiar man behind counter replied and disappeared into the kitchen. Soon a different man wearing a grease-stained apron came out from the kitchen and placed a dish on the counter without saying anything. Then he went back to the kitchen. I thought that he had to be a kitchen helper, since he didn't know how to deal with a customer. Even though he didn't say anything, the dish was obviously mine, since there was no other customer. I stood up from my table and walked to the counter. The dish contained a big piece of chicken, mashed potato with gravy, and string beans. I took the dish and returned to my table. When I placed the dish on my table, I wondered why it was called "chicken chow mein". Then the side door of the kitchen opened and the kitchen helper appeared. He walked directly to the counter. He looked at the counter,

but he saw nothing on it. He seemed puzzled. He looked
around and yelled at me, "Hey, that's my lunch!"

Mini-Cultures

"Where can I find nose-paper?" I asked.

A young salesgirl seemed to be scared of my odd question asked in heavily accented English. At that time, sight of non-whites was rare in that part of town, even though many foreigners lived there. She just shook her head, no.

It was the late nineteen fifties. I had arrived in the States a few days before. This was my first shopping adventure. I selected a strange store, called Woolworth's, at Central Square in Cambridge, Mass. I didn't dare to enter any other stores because I was afraid that a salesperson might speak to me. I selected Woolworth's because people seemed to shop there without interference from salespersons. Articles with prices marked on them were displayed for inspection. It was my kind of store, but I couldn't find what I came for. I wandered from one aisle to another in vain. I realized that "nose-paper" might not be the right word. I pulled out my Japanese-English dictionary and looked up *hanagami*, the Japanese word for "nose-paper." It indicated that the corresponding word in English was toilet paper. I knew what toilet paper was and it was not nose-paper, but I had no choice. I asked her again, "Toilet paper?" She led me to a stack of toilet paper rolls. It was the wrong item, but it would have to do the job for a while.

The next day in school I sought out another Japanese student who arrived a few weeks before me. His experience might help me. I asked him, "Where can I buy nose-paper?"

"You cannot buy it here, because Americans don't use nose-paper. They blow their noses with handkerchiefs."

"Yuk. That's unsanitary."

"Yes, it is. Did you ever see a movie in which Clark Gable took out his nose-paper from a back pocket and blew his nose?" he concluded his advice.

Later on the same day, I saw an American classmate blowing his nose with paper, not a handkerchief. He told me it was Kleenex and I could buy it at Woolworth's.

Inconvenience in daily life was a minor problem compared with school work. As I expected, I had trouble understanding English conversations, but I had no problem with reading comprehension, especially in the field of engineering. I had a better grasp of the technical vocabulary than an average classmate did because of my five-years of industrial experience. Nevertheless, I had a difficult time figuring out instruction sheets for lab classes.

For instance, they said: Set up Dumont. Press the start button of Sanborn. Adjust Slidac. When Weston reaches 5 A, record numbers from Foxboro and Honeywell. Then enter the data into Flex-o-writer for future analysis.

That didn't tell me anything. I checked my dictionaries for these strange words; Dumont, Sanborn, and so on. I consulted not only Japanese-English, but also Merriam Webster's Collegiate. I couldn't find any entries for them. I read textbooks repeatedly but I couldn't figure out their meanings.

I attended the first lab class and found out that they were designations for equipment. They were manufacturers' names, trade/brand names or models. The only way I learned them was to go to the lab, peer through every piece of equipment, and find items having corresponding labels such as Dumont, Sanborn, etc.

Dumont turned out to be a cathode ray tube, or CRT, similar to a television screen for observing electronic signals. If the instructor had used the generic name, CRT or Braun tube (after its inventor), I could instantly have recognized the equipment. Since a typical instruction sheet included more than a dozen of these names, I wasted uncountable minutes trying to find the right equipment, just in preparation for an experiment before I could start it. That left me little time to perform the actual experiment and to think about its real meaning.

I assumed that the cause of my problem was the transition between two cultures: from Japanese to American. I was wrong. I attended a social gathering of Japanese students, where we shared troubles and difficulties of our lives in the United States. A guy from Mechanical Engineering said, "Around here, people use 1020, instead of S-2522-6."

"What are you talking about?" I asked him.

"These are types of sheet metal," he told me scornfully.

A loud mouthed Electrical Engineering student boasted, "Electrical engineering is universal and no problem here. 2N136 is 2N136, in the U.S. or in Japan."

I didn't risk asking what was 2N136, but I had to join the pissing contest, "My field is lucky, everything is brand new and moving fast. I don't need to worry about old stuff. LOX supersedes H2-O2 and cryogenic replaces hydrocarbons." That shut everyone up.

This was not Japanese vs. American cultures, but enclaves of professional cultures. They used their own vocabularies and conventions, incomprehensive to outsiders.

During the spring vacation, I went to Washington for sightseeing with two of my Japanese friends. En route, we often ate submarine sandwiches, a favorite meal among Japanese students. Soon we discovered that submarines disappeared and became hero sandwiches. They were again transformed into Cuban sandwiches.

I finally realized that every community, which could be cultural, geographical, ethnic, or even generational, has its own special vocabularies and conventions, namely a "mini-culture." These could be slang, favored brand names, local stores, dialects, music, TV programs, sports, etc. Each community was unique and different, so it had its own mini-culture. In order to learn these mini-cultures, I had to live in the community and submerge myself in it. This meant that whenever I moved from one community to another, I had to relearn a new mini-culture.

In 1998, I retired and moved into a small retirement community, located in Indiantown, an unincorporated area in central Florida. Four-fifths of the town's population is Latino farm workers, some of them illegal immigrants. Once I settled in the new home, I wanted to buy the green tea which I had formerly gotten in Stop and Shop, Star Market, or Johnny's Food Mart in Massachusetts. I asked Pamela, a town old timer. She said to try Rines first, then Publix or Winn-Dixie in Stuart. It took me several minutes of a question and answer session before I could comprehend the full meaning of her answer. I had forgotten how tough it was to become acquainted with a new mini-culture. I needed a break from the tension. Should I have a glass of Sam Adams Beer? No. I wasn't in Boston anymore. I was in Indiantown, I had to have Corona or Modelo.

What is it?

"Beautiful! Gorgeous! Exotic!" Newlyweds, my wife, Ann, and I admired the present from my mentor, Professor Chang. It was an oriental antique or replica, eighteen-inches high, twenty-four inch wide, black cast-iron spherical container with two ring handles on opposite sides. A cylindrical copper vessel was suspended inside. Its six-inch diameter iron lid had a grain pattern resembling those on the famous Japanese *Nambu* teapot. The two ring handles of the outer case were almost identical to those of the *Ura-Senke* tea ceremony kettle. A two-inch high supporting rim for the internal container had geometric patterns of nested squares appearing on the rims of bronze ceremonial wine containers from the twelfth century BCE Yin dynasty in China. The outer case had two big openings in opposing positions. The flattened-heart shape holes were identical to those in large incense burners in Japanese temples. The unique feature of the antique was its handle supports. Both were carved as human faces, one man and the other woman. The cast iron object had three thick feet, each two inches high.

We placed the gift at the center of the dining table in our new apartment and admired it every day. Guests praised its grace and balance as well as apparent antiquity. The lingering question for us was, "What is it?" We suspected it was a good reproduction, but we wanted to know the usage of the original item, at least its origin. We guessed it had to be Japanese or Chinese, because I was

Japanese and Professor Chang was Chinese. To the best of my knowledge it was not Japanese. I had researched it in the university library to make sure it wasn't an obscure Japanese item. So we postulated it had to be Chinese, but again I failed to identify the item in reference books in the library.

We were embarrassed every time some guest asked what it was. After three months of continuous annoyance from many inquiries and unsatisfied curiosity, I built up courage and visited Professor Chang in his office. "Professor, my wife and I like your wedding present very much and admire it every day. However, I have to admit my ignorance of the identity of the item. Please tell me what it is."

"Ha, ha, it is an authentic reproduction of an ancient Japanese kitchen utensil. When I visited Hong Kong last summer, I bought it in the gift shop of The Oriental Museum, especially as a wedding present for my faithful Japanese assistant."

"Thank you sir, I should be ashamed of my ignorance. That makes sense. It has some resemblance to the portable charcoal stove, which Americans often call Hibachi," I said.

In reality, I wasn't satisfied at all with his explanation. I knew it was not Japanese. Since the Chinese museum people identified it as Japanese, it was definitely not Chinese, either. Then what? The mystery thickened but I didn't have any ideas. So we had to continue admiring this mysterious object, which attracted attention from our dinner guests and became a focus of conversation.

Several years later, my wife insisted on inviting Doctor Watanabe, a notable Japanese visiting astrophysicist from my office. She thought we owed him a dinner invitation out of kindness since his wife and children went back to Japan and he was living alone. I wasn't too keen on associating with him because of his arrogance and obnoxiousness, but due to her insistence, I invited him to dinner.

Most of the conversation was carried out in Japanese between him and me. Because my wife didn't understand Japanese, he ignored her most of time, like a typical old-fashioned Japanese man. Doctor Watanabe used English only when he had to recite obligatory pleasantries to my wife. Most of our conversation was his lecture to me about the decadence of American culture. He said that I had made a big mistake to marry an American woman. At least I should send our children to schools in Japan, or they would be spoiled by American culture. That was one of the reasons he sent his family back to Japan even though he would have to stay another year in the United States.

I wanted to terminate our uncomfortable conversation as soon as possible, and send him home. Somehow my wife didn't get my subtle signal and innocently pointed out the centerpiece. "Doctor Watanabe, do you know what this is? We received this from Yashi's mentor, Professor Chang as our wedding present, but we can't figure out what it is. Professor Chang said it is a Japanese cooking utensil, but Yashi didn't believe it is."

Doctor Watanabe would never miss a chance to show his knowledge and superiority over us lower class people, "Well, well," he scornfully murmured while composing his reply in English, "Mrs. Nozawa."

"Please call me, Ann, Doctor Watanabe," my wife said.

"Yes, Ann, I read about this object in a classic Buddhist book a long time ago. It was a Buddhist mummy maker."

"Mummy maker? You are kidding!"

"Ann, a Japanese samurai gentleman, such as I am, doesn't joke about such things. This object is an obvious miniature replica of the mummy maker. The real mummy maker, which is a sacred treasure of the *Shingon* temple, is taller than a standing man. When a determined monk decides to become a flesh statue of the Buddha, namely a mummy in modern terms, they use this mummy maker. The procedure was a most sacred ceremony and rarely performed; according to the record, perhaps once every fifty to one hundred years."

"Mummy-making is illegal under modern law, but Buddhists would perform the procedure as the occasion arises," Doctor Watanabe explained. "The whole process takes three years. The candidate monk at first starts with special diets. He reduces his intake of food and eliminates at first carbohydrates, then fat, by eating only vegetable protein such as dried tofu and dried nuts. He reduces consumption of water, too. Eventually he becomes a skinny person made of bone and skin. Throughout this process, he sits in the meditation posture and recites prayers. After completion of the first year's preparation, he is transferred to the center chamber, equivalent to the copper cylinder of this replica. The chamber is just large enough for a man to sit inside. After a ceremony, the chamber is sealed at the top. The chamber has many small holes for air to circulate and discharge bodily waste. Meanwhile the monk continuously recites prayers. As long as his prayer voice is audible, assistants insert two dried nuts and an ounce of water every day.

"Seven days after his prayers have ceased, a major ceremony is performed and the top lid will be opened. If the monk has stayed more than one year in the chamber, he will become a flesh statue of the Buddha. His general appearance will be preserved. There will be no unpleasant odor. Then his flesh statue will be placed at the center of the temple and worshipped by many followers.

"If the monk didn't survive long enough and some flesh remains, then his remains will be left in the chamber and be repacked with dry tealeaves. The lid will be sealed again, and a charcoal fire placed under the container to burn for forty-nine days. After the forty-ninth day, the body will be re-examined. This process continues until the remains are completely mummified and it becomes a flesh statue of the Buddha," he concluded. His story was entertaining, but I didn't believe it at all. I knew the process of making a flesh statue of the Buddha.

Suddenly Dr. Watanabe showed his true nature, and said, "I have to point out to you that the person who gave this had bad intentions."

"Why do you say that?" I raised my voice.

"Nozawa-*kun*, you know that Buddhism is associated with funerals, not marriage, don't you?" he asked.

"Yes, marriage ceremonies in Japan are performed by Shinto priests," I answered.

"See, the person who gave this present is hexing it," he insisted.

For a long time, we regretted the dinner invitation to him. We didn't believe what he said, but his comments influenced our thinking. The mysterious antique moved from the center of our dining table to the knick-knack shelf. Our contact with my mentor, Professor Chang, diminished and ceased. Much later we learned from a newspaper obituary of his death.

One day in the late eighties, Mr. Atkinson from our church had dinner at our house. He turned out to be an anthropologist, specializing in Asian cultures. He noticed the mysterious antique on our knick-knack shelf and said, "You have an interesting object here. Where did you get this?"

"It was a wedding gift from my mentor, Professor Chang," I said.

"He must be a thoughtful person to select this for a wedding present," he said.

"Why is that?" I responded.

"This is a prized wedding cooking pot. The original form started in the fourth century in Southern Korea and the Kyushu region of Japan. The same tribe inhabited both areas at that time, even though they were separated into different countries in the sixth century. It was a royal ceremonial cooking pot but it became wedding cookware in noble families. The custom of wedding cookware later shifted to the North. At present, the custom survives only in Northern Korea and Northeastern China. We don't know how they used it in ancient time, but the present use of this utensil is interesting. A newlywed couple retires into their bedroom with this utensil. The bottom part holds red-hot charcoal. The center part holds the wedding meat, that of a specially bred dog. Local people believe that the meat will heat up bodies even on the coldest night. In other words, they believe in its aphrodisiac effect. Also, the dog is a symbol of fertility. On the wedding night the newlywed couple cook and eat together this special animal in their bedroom before they go to bed," he explained.

No wonder Professor Chang didn't tell me the details! He said that it was ancient Japanese cookware. He knew that the Japanese had `stopped eating meat since the seventh century when Buddhism was introduced in Japan, even though my generation enjoyed eating meat. When he gave us this present he assumed that I knew its significance. When he realized my ignorance, he was afraid that I might be repelled by the idea of cooking dog meat, even though it was the best wedding present of all we received.

We were sorry not to express our sincere thanks to Professor Chang because of our ignorance. He was a thoughtful and kind person, contrary to the opinion of Doctor Watanabe who tried to intimidate and mislead us with his story.

The mysterious oriental antique has returned to the center of our dining table. Sometimes we entertain dinner guests with tales of mummy maker and wedding cookware, but omit telling what kind of meat was cooked in the pot.

Car of the Future

"**Y**ou are fired as of now, Mr. Nozawa," Professor Hunter declared in an ice-cold voice. I had been working for the past nine month as a control system analyst for his Army funded project, called "Car of the future." The car was a single-seater less than 2 feet wide and speed capability of more than 150 mph even on a curve without danger of flipping over. The secret was the tilting wheel mechanism that could automatically compensate for centrifugal force during a turn, so that any driver without the training of a motorcycle rider could operate it with the speed and maneuverability of a motorcycle.

At that time, I was a graduate student for Master's degree with a major in control theory. When I was ready to take the job, my fellow graduate students warned me that I should not select a thesis subject in a gadget-making project. Such a project could fail and I would not be able to complete my thesis. I ignored all these warnings because I was so excited to be involved in the development of the new car of the future as well as receiving a pay while working for my thesis. The professor wanted a theoretical analysis which would endorse the soundness of his idea for his project in his report for the Army.

I had just completed my theoretical analysis and presented the result to the Professor on February 21, exactly one week before the deadline for the thesis. My conflict was that I uncovered an inherent danger in the car

design. Under certain conditions such as bumps on the road, the tilting wheel mechanism would become unreliable and unstable. The new car would become dangerous under such conditions and the driver of the car would be thrown out, even though the car itself might not flip over. Our interview was short and bitter.

"Professor Hunter, I don't mind losing my job, but what will happen to my degree? Sir, this report is also my Master's thesis," I appealed to his sympathy.

"I cannot accept a thesis with serous error in it, can I? You will hear from me. Good day, Mr. Nozawa."

I was devastated. Because he was not the type of person to review details of my report or to check all calculations, he would probably hand my report to one of his assistants, usually another graduate student. In my personal opinion, none of his graduate students would be as good as I was in theoretical calculations. So this could be like asking a blind man to critique the "Mona Lisa". My future would be doomed if the result was negative. I would not receive my degree that year. I might have to enroll for another year or two to get a degree. Our wedding planned for after graduation would have to be indefinitely postponed. Since I lost my lob, I would have to find another income source to support further study.

My repeated attempts to contact the professor failed. I looked for him all over the campus. The message I got from his secretary was that he was traveling to secure new funding for his project. Since I couldn't make contact with him, I submitted my thesis at the last minute to department headquarters. The thesis had a new cover sheet, but its contents were identical to my final report to the professor. The thesis cover sheet lacked the endorsement of my thesis adviser, namely the signature of the Professor Hunter. I explained to department headquarters that I couldn't get my professor's endorsement because he was away. The administrative people were sympathetic to my situation and accepted my thesis provisionally, meaning that they would get his signature for me when he came back from his trip, assuming he would be willing to sign it. If he did sign it, then my thesis was considered to be submitted before the deadline. If he would not sign it, then my thesis was considered not to be submitted at all. Once I submitted my thesis, I had nothing to do in the school except to wait for a notice from the department headquarters. I started to look for a job, assuming I would graduate.

Around April 15, I received a formal notice in the mail from department headquarters and I was an official candidate for the Master's degree. My thesis was accepted. Prof. Hunter somehow conceded the correctness of my calculation, or he was just nice enough to pity my situation and signed off my thesis. I didn't care what made him sign it as long as he signed it. I received my Master's degree on May 5 and married Ann on June 4.

Our wedding ceremony was held in the school chapel. My new wife and I made a courtesy visit to my old department. Since the summer vacation had already started, the department was deserted, but I met Joe, an old technician who worked for more than thirty years in the department.

"Yashi, nice to see you. Is this your new wife?" he said.

"Thank you, Joe. Yes, she is my new wife. What's going on in the department nowadays?" I said.

"We are waiting for new funding for the Car of the Future project."

"Do you think Prof. Hunter will get it? The new funding?"

"I don't think so."

"Why?" I asked.

"I will tell you something, just for you. This is supposed to be super secret."

"Ok, my lips are sealed," I replied.

"You know your report? Arthur Mark, the smartest doctoral candidate in the department, reviewed it and agreed with your calculation completely. Because of that, nobody wanted to ride the car when a test rider was needed. Finally the Prof. got so frustrated he rode it himself. Guess what happened next."

"What?" I said

"He was thrown off the car and broke his shoulder."

A Memorable Party

"What is this, may I ask?" Mrs. Bishop pointed to a bowl of yellow gel.

"It's stirred raw egg. You cool your piece of meat by dipping into it. Otherwise the meat might to be too hot to eat," Adam said. I noticed her reluctance and confusion.

"You don't need to use it. Many Westerners don't like it. Here, use this broth for cooling," I pushed another bowl toward her. She gratefully accepted my offer and pushed the bowl of raw egg aside. Dr. Bishop copied her action. After we had placed several pieces of meat and vegetable into their broth, Dr. Bishop bravely tried to pick up a vegetable by himself with his chopsticks. The piece of vegetable dropped into the stew and boiling hot liquid splashed on the table.

"Dr. Bishop, I think these tongs may be easier for you; even Japanese have trouble picking up vegetables with chopsticks," I said. Once the initial difficulties were over, our *sukiyaki* party at the home of Dr. Bishop went smoothly.

It had started about a month ago. Adam, Keith and I, the Japanese trio in the Aeronautics and Astronautics Department of the University, had a weekly *sukiyaki* party in Adam's one room apartment. Adam and Keith were not their real names. The trio, the only Japanese in the department, had adopted American names for the convenience of their colleagues. They were visiting researchers and I was a graduate student in the department.

Sukiyaki is one of few traditional Japanese dishes palatable to both Japanese and Westerners. It is a stew of meat and vegetables in soy sauce broth with a dash of *sake* wine, cooked in a special flat bottom cast iron pan and served hot. Adam liked *sukiyaki* so much he couldn't bear American life without it. So he asked his wife to ship the heavy *sukiyaki* pan to him from Japan. He also managed to gather necessary ingredients or close substitutes locally. The main ingredient is thinly sliced beef, which none of the local supermarkets or butchers could supply. He discovered a fish store, called Legal Seafood, at Inman Square in Cambridge. The storeowner, George, who had been in Japan as a serviceman, was friendly to Japanese residents. We initially went to there to buy a chunk of tuna fish for *sashimi*. His store actually consisted of two stores side-by-side with different entrances, but connected inside. One was a fish store and the other, a meat store. Adam asked him to slice beef for him for *sukiyaki*. George tried but couldn't slice, since the meat was too soft. Adam suggested he freeze the meat lightly to make it harder and to use a slicing machine. After a few experiments, George succeeded in slicing raw beef thin enough for *sukiyaki*. Ever since, all Japanese people in Boston flocked to his store for tuna chunks and *sukiyaki* beef. He had to expand his store to accommodate this sudden increase in business. George later opened the famous Legal Seafood restaurant chain, but this is another story.

Once Adam had the main ingredient, thinly sliced beef, he went to Chinatown to purchase other ingredients or substitutes. For instance, Chinatown sold Chinese soy sauce, *shiitake* mushrooms, and *daikon* radishes, but didn't have *shirataki* noodles or *negi* leeks. Adam substituted them with Chinese rice noodles and scallions respectively. The result was a spectacular success, so he invited us for a *sukiyaki* dinner.

Despite our busy schedules, ever since that time we had managed to meet once a week on Friday night for *sukiyaki* dinner with exchange of gossip and nostalgic conversation. During one of these dinner parties, Adam and Keith brought up the subject of a thank-you gift for Dr. Bishop, who was the head of the department. Without his help they would not have been able to come to the university.

It was the late fifties; Japan was a semi-closed country, due to a shortage of foreign currency reserve. The Japanese government tightly controlled all foreign travel to save foreign currency, especially long term stays. Both men got special permission for their nine-month stay at the university because of Dr. Bishop's endorsement. Dr. Bishop, often called "the father of inertial guidance," was well-known even in Japan. So the Japanese government reluctantly allowed both to leave Japan and to spend the precious dollar reserve. Adam and Keith felt strongly they were obliged to give an additional gift to Dr. Bishop before their departure in a month or so.

They had already given souvenirs from Japan to Dr. Bishop. Unfortunately what they brought with them for souvenirs were all poor quality products, typical representatives of "made in Japan," even though they were exotic. The new gift had to be something memorable. Anything they might buy here was no good, because it wouldn't be a Japanese product and not memorable. They didn't have extra money to buy an expensive gift. I proposed that we invite him and his wife to a Japanese dinner. It would be memorable for them, since they never had a Japanese dinner before. They thought it was a good idea, but impractical. There was only one Japanese restaurant, Kyoto near Symphony Hall, in the greater Boston area. We agreed the restaurant was too shabby for this purpose and it didn't serve alcoholic drinks, even beer. We were stuck, even though I thought it was a good idea.

"Hey, Adam, you should cook for them. You are a good cook and you have this special *sukiyaki* pan. So, you can offer authentic Japanese *sukiyaki* that no Japanese restaurants can offer," I said.

"Where shall we have the dinner party?"

"How about here?"

"No, I have no table, except this kitchen table, or extra chairs, or dishes or utensils."

"We can rent them, can't we?"

"I think it is too dingy, maybe worse than the Kyoto restaurant."

"How about catering?" I said.

"What is that?"

"It's American equivalent of *demae*, food delivery. We cook *sukiyaki* here and deliver the finished product to Dr. Bishop's house. I can pretend to be a delivery person while you two are visiting there."

"But *sukiyaki* has to be hot."

"Well we can borrow their kitchen to warm it."

Keith, who had been quiet during our discussion said, "Why doesn't Adam cook the whole thing there, if we have to borrow their kitchen?"

We agreed. So Adam made an appointment with Dr. Bishop and got permission for the party in his house. Meanwhile Keith and I were busy preparing authentic ingredients for the party. We drove to a Japanese food store in New York East Side and bought *Kikkoman* soy sauce, *Marukan mirin* cooking wine, *shirataki* noodles, *shiitake* mushroom and *negi* leeks, fat Japanese *daikon* radishes, ten pounds of short grain Japanese rice, and a case of *Kirin* beer. Adam ordered three pounds of special cut beef from George.

One week later we had had our own last *sukiyaki* party at Adam's apartment. We fondly recalled the

success of Dr. Bishop's party. They had never had any
Japanese dishes before. Everyone remembered how Mrs.
Bishop seemed to be pleased. They were impressed with
our effort to make the dish authentic. She had inquired
about all ingredients and method of cooking. She showed
special interest in the *sukiyaki* pan and automatic rice
cooker. It was surely a memorable party for Dr. Bishop
and his wife. It was a memorable party for us, too. We
had never seen the inside of a rich American home,
especially its kitchen. We learned about a few things,
such as dishwasher, timer-controlled baking oven, electric
mixer, and Pyrex pans.

We successfully completed our thank-you party
believing we had accomplished our intended purpose.
They must have had a memorable party, since nowhere in
the U.S. they could have had authentic *sukiyaki*, because
no *sukiyaki* pan was available except at Adam's. We
thought it was a worthwhile enterprise, in spite of trouble.
Besides preparation, we made sure that the kitchen was
sparkling clean before we left. If we had left any soy
sauce spots on top of stove or counter, there might be
permanent stains.

A few years later, long after I left school, I noticed a
large obituary in the Boston Globe. It was for Mrs. Bishop,
a notable Boston high society grande dame, whose
personal kindness and charitable works were famous. As
an example of her kind acts, the article included an
anecdote about poor Japanese students. According to the
article, while her husband, Dr. Bishop, was the head of a
department in the University, three poor Japanese students
in his department were living under tight money
conditions, due to the strict dollar control of the Japanese
government. They especially longed for their native
dishes, because of the unfamiliarity of American dishes
and absence of any Japanese restaurant in Boston at that
time. Furthermore, they couldn't cook any native dishes

since they had no ingredients to cook or kitchen to use. So Mrs. Bishop made arrangements to get the necessary ingredients from New York. Then she invited these poor students and offered them the ingredients and use of her kitchen to cook them. These students cooked the ingredients and enjoyed their long-missed native dishes, which she had shared with them. They were so thankful for her act of kindness, that even today she occasionally receives a thank you note from them. She fondly used to say," It was a memorable party."

Meditation: My Experience

"No women, no alcohol and no smelly vegetables beyond this gate": the sign at the main entrance read. It was a famous Zen temple, *Enkaku-ji* in Japan. We stayed there for the next five days for a manager-training course of my employer, Mutsui Corporation. It seemed an odd place for such a purpose, but the company president believed the spirit of Zen would improve our performance.

The temple was situated at the top of a low mountain with dense woods surrounding it. I felt completely isolated from the noisy hustle-bustle of the modern world. The only sound was the soothing continuous songs of summer cicadas. The air was cool and I could barely see a bright blue sky through the tips of tall cedar trees. A narrow stone path led toward denser woods. For five minutes we walked along the path to an open space in which several large single story wooden buildings stood. All the buildings had a similar structure: Large tiled roofs with recessed walls and raised floors as high as our heads. A middle-aged monk greeted us and escorted the group to a small building hidden behind a larger one, the size of an average tool shed. There were no windows in the building. Light came only from the entrance, which had no door. Inside the building, there was a narrow U-shaped raised platform along three walls. The platform was made of hardwood, shining and black from its long usage. There was no furniture or decoration inside.

"This is a meditation hut. You will spend most of your time here during your stay," the monk explained.

The next morning, a black-robed monk carrying a long flat pole, just like a small oar, guided us to the hut. We took off our shoes and climbed to the waist-high platform. He taught us how to sit correctly.

"Sit with legs crossed at the front, straight back without leaning on the wall, and facing toward the center of the room. Hands hang naturally and rest on the legs. Both hands should touch each other, weaving fingers together with palms up. Both hands should form a sort of a pocket between the legs. Close your eyes, but you must not doze. Breathe slowly. No sound and no movement are allowed. Just sit still. Most importantly, don't think anything, just sit still, and let your mind take care of itself. This is the meditation," he said. We practiced the meditation nine hours a day for the next four days: one hour before breakfast, three after breakfast, three after lunch and two after supper.

At the beginning, I had difficulty sitting still. My legs became numb, my face got itchy, and my back started aching. Whenever I made a slight movement, the monk yelled "Kha!" and hit my shoulder with the long oar-like pole. The blow did not hurt, but did startle me. It produced a slapping sound loud enough to wake the dead.

For a while, the only thing I could think about was how to sit still for an hour. Once I mastered that part of the technique, I had to fight against dozing. By the second day, I was accustomed to sitting still without dozing. The next challenge was my wandering mind. I started to think of various things: Why does the company want us to do this ridiculous act? What is my girlfriend doing now? And so on. Somehow, the monk knew I was thinking something.

"Forget everything and make your mind empty!" he whispered.

By the end of the third day, I felt calm and refreshed. Maybe it was an effect of the meditation or maybe the result of an empty stomach. Every meal was simple and meager: Two bowls of rice, one bowl of soup and five pieces of pickle. I was hungry the first two days. The instruction was to eat to only seventy percent of your stomach capacity and prevent a full stomach. Eventually I became accustomed to it and didn't feel hunger. Human adaptation was amazing.

The last day of the training, we had a sermon from the top monk of the temple. He said that the Zen Sect of Buddhism was originated in China by a monk called Dharma in the sixth century and Monk Eisai brought it to Japan in the early twelfth century. The essence of Zen was that the truth of the universe would be found only by direct experience of an individual through a sitting meditation. The goal of Zen was to achieve an eternal peace of mind. To achieve eternal peace of mind one must abandon all worldly thoughts. Only we and nobody else would achieve our peace of mind, so we had to practice our meditation. Zen meditation was difficult to master and only a few people had achieved true peace of the mind. According to legend, Monk Dharma meditated for nine years continuously. When he achieved his eternal peace of mind, he didn't have any hands and legs any more. During the long period of meditation, his extremities rotted away. For ordinary people like us, it was difficult to abandon all desires and thoughts, but we could temporarily empty our minds by practicing meditation. Once we emptied our minds and abandoned our greed and desires, we could do anything well. We couldn't control our environment, but we could control our reaction to the environment. An empty mind could make a right decision, which would control our destiny. "When you face a difficult situation, first meditate a while, empty your mind, and make a right decision," he concluded.

His speech was short but puzzling. I knew that Zen was sophisticated and difficult to understand for an average person like me. My best interpretation of his speech was that I had to empty my mind before I could make a good decision.

When we returned to our company, our human resources manager wanted us to submit an essay about our training course. I struggled about what I should write. I meditated. My mind went completely blank and I forgot everything. I couldn't write anything. It seemed that I had really mastered the true spirit of Zen meditation.

Part Two
In Aerospace Industry

Not At My Expense

W ho would imagine that a minor snowfall would cause me seven years of frustration and inconvenience? The time was the early nineteen sixties; I was managing a field-support team on a satellite project for a laboratory of the federal government. My responsibility was to guide both prototype and flight hardware successfully through vigorous qualification and certification tests. They conducted most of the tests in the Federal Test Center located in a suburb of Washington D.C. I spent most of my time in the facility, even though both my home and my home office were located in Massachusetts. While I worked in the center, I lived in a motel in Washington area and commuted there with a rental car.

One winter morning, we had an unexpected snowfall in Washington D.C. The snow started in the morning after I left my motel and kept getting worse while I was driving. When I approached the center, I noticed a long line of cars starting at the traffic signal near the main entrance. The line hardly moved even when the signal changed. The signal was located at the top of a hill, so waiting cars were sitting on a slope. When they were ready to move, many couldn't proceed. They spun wheels without traction. Snow is rare in the area. Most of cars had no snow tires and the road was not sanded. Many cars had to be pushed by people to move. Progress of the line was slow. Meanwhile snow was still falling.

At first, the wiper removed snow from my windshield, but more accumulated. My view was blocked by the snow. I looked for an ice scraper in the glove compartment, but nothing was there. I searched for a potential substitute. The only thing I found was a car pass which was placed on the dashboard. It was made of a piece of hard plastic. I used the car pass to scrape the snow off the windshield. In the next half hour I repeated the action numerous times.

When I reached the main gate, I was stopped by a guard, who asked for my car pass. I looked for it inside the car but couldn't find it.

When I requested the reissue of my car pass, they told me that I need to file a loss report and to get an acknowledgement letter from my supervisor about my loss of government property. Immediately I called my home office and asked my boss to write the letter. He said no and insisted that I should get it from the test center where I was working when I lost the pass. I went to the liaison office which had been coordinating our job at the center. They said that I had to ask for the acknowledgement letter from the project office rather than from the liaison office. I went to the project office. They said that they couldn't issue such a letter and I had to receive it from my home office. This shift of responsibility went on week after week.

Since I didn't have my car pass, I had to check in the guard house every morning to get a visitor's pass. It meant that a guard had to call the center employee whom I specified and the called person had to agree that he was expecting me. Even though someone from my team was there twenty-four hours a day, they had no authority to clear me. It was inconvenient and inefficient for me and for other project people.

I couldn't understand why they refused to write a simple acknowledgement letter, so I asked a trusted friend who was a career federal employee.

Instead of answering my question, he asked me, "Yashi, are you in civil service?"

"No, I am not," I replied.

"Unless you are in civil service, it is difficult to understand," he said.

According to him, there were two types of federal employees; one was civil service and other private payroll. Private payroll employees, of whom I was one, were hired for a specific project only and their employment would last as long as the project was funded. In the case of civil service, their employment was life time guaranteed. However, any minor mistake or negative personnel record would hinder their career advancement. As a result, a civil service employee tends to avoid taking responsibility which might produce a negative result. Writing the acknowledgement letter for my loss of government property was considered to be a negative point for the author's career record.

Once I realized the underlying operational principle of the civil service employees I gave up the notion of getting my second car pass. I stopped at the guard house every morning for the entire seven years of my stay at the test center.

One time I was awakened by a frantic call from my team about one o'clock in the morning. I quickly got up, dressed, and hurried to the test center. At the guard house, a guard tried to call an employee who could vouch for me. He couldn't find anybody even though he tried more than twenty-five people. All the daytime employees were not there. I frantically searched my brain for anyone who might be there at that time of a day. I recalled Dr. Rose, an astronomer, who often came and stayed all night to observe stars. I barely knew him, but we had chatted a couple of times. Luckily he remembered who I was and cleared me to enter the center. Fortunately for the project, I arrived in time to fix the problem and to prevent a major disaster.

Shortly after the successful conclusion of our project, the project office held a celebration ceremony at the center. All project people, including myself, were invited. When I arrived there, a guard had trouble locating the right person to vouch for me. All project personnel were in auditorium for the celebration. The guard said that the vouching person had to be in his office, otherwise anyone could impersonate the person. So calling the auditorium number was not an acceptable alternative. He tried a dozen people but none was in their office. Eventually I gave up and went home.

According to the story I heard later, I was one of the few recipients of the certificates of merit which were handed out during the ceremony. I wish they had straightened out my car pass, instead of giving me the certificate, which had no discernable value for me as a private payroll employee. For me, the end of the project was the end of my employment. Apparently receiving the certificate of merit was a big thing for civil service employees. I understood that my supervisors, both from project office and home office, received promotion based on exceptional contribution of their subordinate, namely me, toward the project.

Joe's Superstition

" Joe, what secret are you holding back? You were supposed to teach Keith everything you know," Fredrick Kaltenstahl, Director of Research and Development, Westinghouse Corporation, was interrogating Joe Harrison, a former research technician.

"No secret, sir. I didn't hold back anything. I taught Keith everything. I thought he was doing fine," Joe was visibly upset.

"Keith couldn't produce the same tube as you did. Sensitivity of his tubes was only one tenth of yours. We think you did something different from the way specified in the procedure. What is it?" Kaltenstahl accused Joe.

"Nothing, sir. You saw how I made a tube. I have no reason to hold back anything. I want to help you and Keith more than anyone else, but I don't know why he couldn't make the same tube as I did. We used the same materials, the same equipment and the same procedure."

"Joe, think, think harder! You had to have done something beyond the specified procedure," Kaltenstahl pressed harder.

After a few minutes of silence, Joe said, "Yes, there was one thing I did extra."

"What was it?" Kaltenstahl excited.

"I said prayers during the sealing process."

"Prayers! Nonsense," Kaltenstahl screamed.

"Fredrick," I interrupted.

"This will not lead us anywhere. I believe in Joe and Keith. If there is a secret, Joe himself doesn't know it. The

37

only way to find it out is to observe their processes and compare them for differences."

It was the early nineteen sixties. We were building the first astronomical satellite, but there was no sensitive enough television camera tube to see stars. We made a three million dollar contract with Westinghouse to develop the camera tube for us. The research and development phase was successfully completed after two years of struggle. The contract proceeded to the production phase. Around that time, Westinghouse had implemented a major reorganization and closed down the research laboratory in Pittsburgh, which had handled our contract and moved the production to the Elmira plant in New York State. Joe, who had been exclusively making camera tubes, retired and his job was shifted to Keith from Elmira. The transition seemed going smoothly at first, but later we discovered that all tubes produced at Elmira had inferior sensitivity. We needed minimum twenty high sensitivity tubes, for our project, but we had none after we consumed materials for more than 150 tubes. So I, as the chief engineer of the satellite project, called an emergency meeting to find out what was going on.

We installed two high speed movie cameras to record the sealing process. A television camera tube was a type of vacuum tube and the sealing was the most crucial process in all production steps. Several observers, including Kaltenstahl and I, gathered around movie cameras. Ten unsealed but otherwise completed camera tubes were neatly lined up on the white Formica covered table. These tubes were the size of the arm of a five-year old kid. At the middle of the arm, a small branch, size of an index finger of the kid, was sticking perpendicularly. The branch was a glass conduit which would be connected to a vacuum pump later.

Joe started first. He picked up one of the tubes by its tail end and carefully placed it on a jig, which consisted of two separate semi cylindrical receptacles. He rotated the tube around its axis to inspect the inside. We could tell how much he rotated the tube by observing the position of the branch. He started out the branch at the horizontal position and rotated it clockwise. Then he overshot slightly and corrected by rotating it counterclockwise until the branch became horizontal again. He might be nervous, because many people were watching him. He picked up the rubber hose from a vacuum pump and connected it to the branch. He started the pump, which made typical compressor like noises. We watched a needle of the vacuum gage which progressed to 1, 2, etc. As the vacuum increased, the sound of the pump changed. When the vacuum gage indicated 5, he switched the pump to a high vacuum device, which was much quieter. We could hardly hear any sound. Joe closed his eyes and seemed listening the whispering sound. When the gage pointed at 10, the target value, he opened eyes and picked up a gas burner which was just like a welder's torch and lit it. He adjusted the flame to a certain size and color. Then he placed the tip of frame about one inch from the glass conduit and heated it. When the glass became red color, he took big pliers, pinched the red glass, and sealed the connection to the vacuum device. He put back pliers, picked up big scissors, and snipped off the glass. He heated the end of glass conduit again and made it smooth. He repeated the process for four more tubes. The next was Keith's turn. He did almost exactly same as Joe did, but he was eager and more precise. He didn't make any mistake. He didn't close his eyes during high vacuum device operation, he was eagerly watching the needle of the vacuum gage. As soon as it reached 10, he picked up the gas burner. He was neater and more efficient than Joe, I thought.

One week later when all sensitivity data were presented we confirmed our fear. Joe's tubes consistently had higher sensitivity than Keith's ones. We watched the movie film repeatedly to discover differences. Differences were Joe's overshoot of a rotation and closing of his eyes. We asked Joe why he did those things. Joe said that he didn't know why, probably just from force of habit. He had been doing them for past 30 years and believed that if he didn't, he would produce inferior tubes. He also added, "I always prayed before opening my eyes."

"Did you tell those habits to Keith?" I asked.

"Yes, but Keith said it was a superstition and laughed at me," Joe said.

We had heated a discussion whether those minor differences would affect the tube sensitivity or not. All Westinghouse people, including several vacuum tube researchers and production experts, thought no effect. I also didn't think of any reason to believe those minor differences would improve the sensitivity, but I was desperate. So, I insisted that we should incorporate those minor differences into the formal manufacturing procedure.

Someone said, "Prayer, too?"

"Yes, but not as a prayer. It will be a 5 second wait period after the gauge reaches the target level. Praying or not is optional to each operator," I replied.

I wished and hoped for, but I was surprised when it really happened. The tube sensitivity was drastically improved after we adopted those changes.

Later Westinghouse discovered that the tubes made with those changes had less moisture content, by 2 parts per billion, compared to tubes without those changes. Apparently this small amount of moister affected the sensitivity of camera tubes. Joe had the secret of the sealing process, which he discovered 30 years ago. Nobody, including Joe himself, knew its significance. We simply called it Joe's superstition, but Joe was finally vindicated with scientific data only after he was forced to retire.

East is East...

Prof. Watanabe, the distinguished Japanese astrophysicist, walked into my small office at Harvard-Smithsonian Institute. He contributed to the earlier US space programs by perfecting orbit calculations for artificial satellites. He and I worked in the same organization, but we had no social contact. In academic institutions like Harvard-Smithsonian, people without Ph.D. and tenure tend to be regarded as sub-humans. I worked there as an engineer, building an astronomical satellite.

When two Japanese meet, right away they have to establish a social pecking order. I said "Have a seat, Watanabe-*san*. Why do I have the honor of receiving you in my humble office?"

He pretended not to notice my mode of address and said, "How are you, Nozawa-*kun*?" Well, this settled our hierarchical positions. He placed me at an inferior position by using "*kun*" instead of the equal level "*san*." Because of my dislike of this kind of social protocol, I had avoided socializing with other Japanese residents. In the middle sixties, only a few hundred Japanese families lived in the greater Boston area. They clustered mostly in Japanese communities and rarely had social contacts with their American neighbors. Dr. Watanabe lived with his wife and son in such a community.

He said, "What are you working on now, the same satellite project? When will it be launched?"

"It was scheduled for July 1966, about ten months from now, but we expect another delay of several months."

"Well, frequent delays are inevitable in any space programs, aren't they? How long have you been working on this project?"

"About four years," I wondered where this conversation was heading. He would never have visited me for chitchat.

"Did you come from Japan to join the project?" He inquired.

"No, no, I was here a couple of years before that," I said.

"So you have been here six years."

"Actually, seven years to be exact."

"So you know lots about American customs, right?"

"Well, some. I learned a lot from my wife."

"That's right, your wife is American, isn't she? Then you must know why Americans can drink so much alcohol without getting drunk."

"No, I don't." Many upper echelon Japanese want to show off their superiority by telling a story which they believe lower class people wouldn't know.

"The French drink wine, the Germans drink beer, the English drink ale, the Scotch drink whisky and the Irish drink everything. Americans are mixture of all of them, so they prefer cocktails or punch. In their ancestors' land, people start drinking alcohol instead of water almost immediately after weaning because their native land has undrinkable water. So their strong resistance to alcohol is genetic. Fortunately, we have good drinkable water in Japan, so we take alcohol occasionally for social reasons only. Furthermore Japanese children and women don't drink alcohol at all. If they take any alcohol, they will get sick."

"Oh, so that is the reason Americans never get drunk!" I said to show my respect toward him.

"Do you know I have a four-year-old son in kindergarten? We received an invitation to a birthday party from one of his classmates. According to the invitation, alcoholic drinks will be served at the party. I know Americans like drinks, but at a birthday party for four-year-old children? They are crazy! My wife and I wondered what should we do. I said no to the party, but my son wanted to go. My wife suggested that I ask you, since you know more about American customs."

"Well, I never heard of serving alcoholic drinks to four-year-olds. I believe it's illegal to serve alcohol to minors. It must be a misunderstanding. How did you get the idea that they would serve alcohol at the party?"

"In the letter we received. Here, see for yourself." He handed me a sheet of paper. It said that because of a recent incident in the kindergarten when one child had a strong allergic reaction to peanut butter, all parents of children attending the party were asked to inform the mother hosting the party of all potential allergies to food and drinks to be served there. It listed milk, coke, ginger ale, root beer, and Hawaiian punch as the drinks being served.

When I saw it, I could hardly control myself. I really wanted to laugh at him, but I didn't want him to lose face. So I answered him. "This parent is very considerate. A son of one of my colleagues was allergic to Hawaiian punch and he always got nosebleeds when he drank it. Also I myself am allergic to milk. I don't know whether your son has an allergy to any of these drinks or not. So the safest way is to test your son before going to the party. Let your wife go to a supermarket and buy a bottle each of these drinks and give your son a small amount of each drink. In Massachusetts, supermarkets are not allowed to sell alcoholic beverages, so I don't believe these drinks contain alcohol. I know their names are confusing. When I was hospitalized for my hip injury a couple of years ago, a nurse asked me whether I would have a glass of ginger ale. I yelled, 'No, no, I don't want any alcohol. It's bad for my wound'. She explained to me that it was sweet carbonated water with an herbal flavor. We studied English at least ten years in Japanese schools, but we learned just language, not the cultural context of the language. This real life stuff often confuses us." I hoped I had given him the necessary information without making him lose face.

"But ale, beer, and punch are alcoholic drinks, aren't they?

"Yes, they are, but they changed their nature when they added adjectives and became Ginger Ale, Root Beer and Hawaiian Punch."

"It's ridiculous, illogical and stupid," he declared.

"Sorry Watanabe-*san*, I designed a satellite but not the English language"

Mr. Silver, Chief of Quality Control

Cold water ran down my back even though I was wearing the hot "bunny suit." There was a black speck, smaller than a grain of rice, on the floor of the clean room below the "wash tub," the mounting plate for our space telescopes. I looked at the speck. It was a flake of black paint.

The time was the nineteen-sixties. It was supposed to be a ceremonial occasion for our space telescope project. We were building the first space telescopes, capable of taking digital video pictures of stars. After many failures and setbacks, we had reached a major milestone.

I would sign the acceptance paper for the wash tub as representative of the Cambridge Institute. Mr. Silver, chief of quality control for all NASA astronomy satellite programs, greeted me by saying, "Yashi, you know how important this occasion is for us and also for you. Astronomy satellite projects have had a difficult time. We know your Institute was the first to enter space astronomy, so we expected to confront new challenges. NASA has limited funds and many competing projects. Your project was a frequent target for cancellation. I am glad we finally reached this milestone."

He continued, "By the way, our team of quality control experts, including myself, has inspected the wash tub and accepted it. So you can sign the acceptance paper now and we can start the official celebration."

"Mr. Silver, believe me. I am aware of where our project stands and the importance of today's event. I don't expect any problem, but I have to see the wash tub in order to carry out my responsibility. Please excuse me, I will go into the clean room and will inspect it," I said.

The clean room was a climate controlled sealed room with filtered air flowing ceiling to floor in order to create a dust-free environment. All satellite related items were stored and assembled in the clean room to avoid dust contamination, a source of failure in space. Every person entering had to wear a bunny suit made of lint free white fabric; go through an air shower stall; and walk over a sticky pad. People tried to avoid entering the clean room because it was cumbersome and time-consuming.

But there was our six-foot diameter giant black wash tub. I examined every surface inside and out, discovering several bare spots in the paint. I lightly tapped the wash tub and several tiny particles fell down.

I thought about the possibility of rejecting the wash tub and its consequences: a setback of six months and several hundred thousand dollars. We were already eighteen months behind. It might even mean project cancellation, which would cause loss of my job. If it were twelve months ago, I would take the consequences, but not now. I had a three month old baby and had bought a new house. My wife had quit her job to take care of the baby. The economy was bad and the prospect of another job was remote. I could not afford to lose a job.

The effect of loose paint would be similar to dusty lenses on a camera, so it might not be too serious. I could ignore the problem and accept the wash tub, making everyone happy and letting the project proceed until the next failure.

I called an emergency meeting of our people using the clean room telephone and made a bee-line to a conference room avoiding everyone. The meeting was attended by the project manager, the chief astronomer, and several engineers and managers who represented our subcontractors. All NASA people were excluded.

I presented my findings, mainly to the chief astronomer, hoping he would say we should reject the wash tub. He was wishy-washy and said he could use even fuzzy pictures. He believed maintaining the project was more important than taking a chance on project cancellation. Almost everyone disapproved of the condition of the wash tub, but they would not take a chance on project cancellation by rejecting it. Their conclusion was that the final decision was mine because I had to sign the acceptance paper. I wanted to get their support or helpful suggestions for my decision, but they didn't give me either. So I said, "Thank you for attending this meeting, I can't make up my mind at this moment, but I will after I meditate for ten minutes or so."

In essence everybody cared abou their own job, not the success or failure of the mission. After a few minutes of meditation, I reached my conclusion. I had to live my life with a clear conscience. I should take the course that made me feel good, not compromise out of greed, fear or worry. I rejected the wash tub. Reaction was immediate. Almost everybody was angry and upset. They tried to persuade me to change my mind. I said, "No way I will change my mind. I believe this is the best decision for me, for our project, and for the future of space astronomy."

The next three months were the darkest days of the project history. Every day was a psychological cliff hanger, waiting to hear news of project cancellation. A review committee from NASA headquarters focused on the reason why such a poor quality product passed several layers of quality control inspection by NASA as well as the manufacturer. NASA also reviewed their policy and reconfirmed that the space astronomy project was at the core of unmanned space exploration and must not be neglected. The results of these extensive reviews were a major overhaul of the space astronomy program management team and modernization of project management techniques. NASA management team had a big shakedown. Deadwood was replaced with competent professional managers. Funding for our project increased.

From my point of view, the biggest change was the attitude of the NASA managers. The old managers hated problems and tried to ignore or hide them. But the new managers acknowledge the inevitability of problems because we were opening new technological frontiers.

Immediately after the incident, Mr. Silver retired to Florida with a NASA pension. He enjoyed fishing and playing golf every day. Curiously, all his golf balls were marked with Y, though his name was Robert. He sometimes yelled swear words while hitting a Y ball. According to a rumor, the Y stood for Yashi, who caused his early retirement. When I heard the story, I felt some sense of relief that my decision contributed both to the prosperity of the United States space astronomy program exemplified by the Hubble telescope, and to the well-being of Mr. Silver.

The Memento

"Where are you going, sir?" a uniformed policeman asked us. The blue flashing light on the roof of his car silhouetted him. I couldn't see his face, but I held out three different security passes in my left hand, "To the emergency vehicle parking lot. We are the project team for the satellite." With my right hand I pointed in the direction we were heading. "In case of launch failure, we have to retrieve the satellite quickly." He accepted this explanation.

It was one o'clock in the morning. The sky was clear and there was no moon. We were standing in a small parking lot surrounded by swamp. The only illumination was from the flashing red lights of four fire engines parked in a straight line on the road leading toward the launch pad. I couldn't identify any constellation in the sky. The periodic bright red illumination interfered my vision. I could glimpse moving shadows of tall swamp grasses. The eerie view contrasted with low reassuring humming noises from the fire engines. The Florida night air was damp and warm. Fumes from the engine exhaust were nauseating. Nobody was talking. Everybody was waiting silently. Tension was high, like the skin of an over-inflated balloon. It might burst any moment with the slightest prick of idle conversation.

Suddenly a radio from a fire engine made cracking sounds, "T minus thirty minutes."

49

Someone said, "We will make it this time." I looked toward the launch pad, but I couldn't see anything there. We were three miles away--- the nearest we could be to the launch pad. Thick stands of swamp grass were obscuring our view of the launch pad. I reached for my tape recorder to turn it on. Within thirty minutes I would see and hear the result of my sweat and tears of the past six years. Atlas-Centaur rocket and its crew would launch my 360 million dollar satellite. They had failed me three times. They had to make it this time.

I had wanted to have a memento for this memorable occasion of my life. Security rule prohibited cameras. I had come up with the idea to record sounds of the rocket engine, which would carry my satellite toward the sky. I had brought my portable tape recorder with me.

The radio cracked again, "T minus eighteen minutes, we are in a hold indefinitely."

"Not again", I thought. "This is our last chance. Please help us, God!" I remembered the battery in the tape recorder would last only one hour. I turned off the battery switch.

Shortly after, the radio announced, "Countdown is resuming." Then again, "T minus ten minutes, we are in a hold indefinitely." I cannot recall how many times this "hold-resume" cycle repeated.

The radio clacked and announced the long awaited message, "T minus one minute, we are now in the last built-in hold for five minutes."

My hope was up, "Good, we will make it this time." Once we resumed the countdown, there would be no built-in hold any more, except in a case of a launch abort.

"Countdown resumed. T minus thirty seconds, T minus twenty seconds, T minus fifteen seconds, T minus ten seconds, nine, eight, seven, six, five, four."

My tension was so high that I yelled, "Three". The last launch abort had happened six month ago --- its countdown had gone to T minus three seconds and the rocket failed.

This time the countdown went smoothly, "Three, two, one, ignition, lift off." This time the countdown went smoothly, "Three, two, one, ignition, lift off. We have a lift off." Everybody screamed, "We did it."

I could see a bright streak of light was going up toward the sky. A few seconds later, hundreds of steam locomotives were roaring over our heads. Sudden quietness set in. It was all over. It had lasted only a few seconds. Red flashing lights were off. Headlights were on. Fire engines were leaving. Darkness returned and only starlight was illuminating us. We could barely see each other, but everybody was shaking hands with everybody, "We did it. We did it."

My satellite, the first orbiting astronomical observatory, finally went up. I was so excited that I had forgotten to turn off my tape recorder. My fingers were wandering on the surface of the tape recorder to locate the battery switch. I finally found the switch. It had been off all the time.

Man's Best Friend

P aul the Babbler, a funny guy, was smart but missing something from his head. He was born and raised in a strict Catholic family. He graduated from Boston Latin, an exam high school and entered MIT. He enjoyed the freedom of dorm life. He played pool, drank a lot and dropped out before the end of the freshman year. His ambition was to become a schoolteacher in Boston, but he didn't have the right connections to get the job. He was working for me as a data analyst at that time, the late nineteen-sixties.

He said, "Yashi, do you have any friends in Chinatown?"

"No friends, but a few acquaintances, maybe," I replied.

"Why don't you introduce me to them?"

"Why?"

"I want to be admitted into one of their places."

"Anyone can go to Chinatown. You don't need an introduction."

"I want to go into backrooms, you know, places where I can play."

"Sorry, I don't know anything about such places," I dismissed his question.

"You won't admit it, but I know you have a connection there," he insisted.

"Paul, I really don't know what you are talking about."

"How about if I tell you my secret system for dog first and you give me a name, OK?"

"No, it's not OK. I don't want to hear your secret and I don't know anything about a name."

He started talking about dog against my protests. I hated dogs. One of them bit me when I was a toddler. It took a few seconds for me to figure out what he was talking about. His dog was a racing greyhound. He preferred to bet on canines because they never cheated him. He had been a regular bettor on greyhound races for the past twenty years, making a steady sideline income with his own sure-win system. He never needed to go to a track; he placed bets through friendly neighborhood bookies in order to save time and to avoid taxes.

His story intrigued me but I pretended to be disinterested. I had to maintain my distance from my subordinates. My attitude seemed to encourage him further. Most of his story was mumbo jumbo to me, due to my ignorance on the subject. To the best of my understanding, his secret system was that a winning dog for a race would be the one which had been at the top spots at both the third corner and finish line in the previous race. He collected data from all racetracks in the areas surrounding Boston. He earned ample pocket money every week with the system. He warned me that I shouldn't bet big money; it would change the odds and attract attention from undesired parties.

He was disappointed when he realized I never had connections to Chinese gambling. I sympathized with him for our misunderstanding but I inwardly congratulated myself on my luck. I decided to test his system. A few days later I went to the Raynham-Taunton track to gather data for Wonderland races. (Later, I found out that I had wasted my time. Each greyhound raced on its registered track only.)

I consumed almost half the night making sense out of the program. When I looked at a real race, I couldn't figure out which dog was at the top position at the third corner. They were too fast for me. There were too many names to memorize, more than one hundred for a single night. They sounded strange to me: Ijusplanowinner, OK Troy, Hondo Monopoly, Rock A Dee, etc. I needed further research before using Paul's system. Research paid off. I didn't need to go to the track for data gathering. Racing results, including third corner positions, were printed in racing newspapers.

After a few weeks of preparation, I was ready to try Paul's system. I went to Wonderland carrying a thick notebook. I arrived one hour before the starting time. I needed plenty of time to select winning dogs, comparing names in the program with entries in my notebook. It was a tedious, frustrating job. I wished to access my office computer, a roomful of a three-million-dollar monster. I approached a wagering window and confidently said, "I'd like two dollars, Place on number five."

According to my calculation, dog Number five, named Ernestina, should win the race, but I conservatively bet top or second position. The posted odds for "Place" for Number five was 3-5, namely a pay off of $3.20 for a $2.00 bet. If I bet "Win", the first place only, the payoff would be $5.00 and for "Show", either first, second or third place, the payoff would be $2.40. Win had a higher payoff but was riskier, and the payoff for show was too low. Exotic wagering such as the daily double, Big-Q, Pick 3, Pick-4, Quiniela, Trifecta, and Superfecta had potentially high pay-offs up to $5000, but the probability of a hit was too small for my purpose of steady wins. Also, frankly speaking, they were beyond my comprehension.

An unexpected problem encountered at the track was that I didn't have enough time to select a winning dog before the next race. I had to bet only every other race. I won some and lost some. I wasn't quite sure Paul's system worked, at least not at that time. The atmosphere at the track interfered with my calculation ability. At home a review indicated I gained a net $2.40 for a total $24.00 investment, exactly 10% return. Not bad for a single night's job. Paul's system worked. Theoretically I could make up to $330,735, if I won every single night for a total of 100 sessions. It seemed somehow unreasonable even for me. Obviously Paul was not making that much. Anyway, it was an encouraging sign.

I went the following night and bet all $27.00, the original capital, the winnings from the day before and some change. The result was a net loss of ten dollars, a disaster. I had to win four consecutive nights, in order to regain the original $24.00. The dream of 100 night consecutive wins was shattered along with an early retirement plan using help from man's best friend. My parents were right, "There is no easy money. You have to earn your money with your sweat." I never went back to a dog track again.

Later I learned that Paul had been making steady pocket money from dog races, not from his own bets, but from commissions. He was a runner for a Boston bookie and taking bets from his coworkers. His story about the sure win scheme was the standard approach to lure new customers. I disappointed him, not because I had no connection to Chinatown, but because I didn't show any interest in dog races.

Double or Nothing

I learned the secret from the famous British spy, James Bond, 007, courtesy Ian Fleming, a scheme to win at casino blackjack. It was in the early 60's while I was working at Harvard-Smithsonian Observatory. We had a new project: to observe the moon through the Arecibo radio telescope, the world's largest. It had been built in a natural geological formation, a semi-spherical ditch more than 1000 feet in diameter. The inside surface of the ditch was covered with steel mesh, which constituted a parabolic reflective surface of radio waves. I was excited at the possibility of using this world-class observational instrument, but I had another source of excitement, too. Because Arecibo was located in a rural area of Puerto Rico, we had to take a small airplane taxi from San Juan, the noted resort city. The airline schedule required us to stay overnight at a hotel in the city, which was famous for its casino, on our return trip. My hidden agenda for this research trip was to test my luck in the casino. I was a scientist and not a gambler, but I was interested in the probabilistic theory of James Bond's scheme. I wanted to test his theory by myself.

Will and I arrived at the hotel in late afternoon. Will was an elderly senior astrophysicist from Arizona who had hired me as his assistant to run the actual radio telescope observation. After supper, he suggested we to go to the hotel casino, as I had hoped. I explained my plan to test James Bond's theory. My plan was quite simple: starting out with a modest sum, say twenty dollars of my own money, I would stick to James Bond's scheme. If I could double the money before tomorrow morning, I would prove his theory. If I lost the entire twenty dollars before tomorrow morning, the theory would appear to be wrong or at least impractical. Will was enthusiastic. He and I walked into the casino area. A well-dressed gentleman, a gatekeeper, stopped us. He refused to admit us into the casino. He said that we had to wear neckties and Will was not dressed properly. Will dressed like a typical Southwestern gentleman. He had a 3-inch diameter silver and turquoise medallion with a thunderbird design on a black string tie, instead of a conventional necktie. Will argued with him that the medallion cost more than five thousand dollars, far more than any necktie, but the gatekeeper didn't budge an inch. Will was disgusted with the whole situation. I suggested to Will that we should return to our rooms, but he encouraged me to continue my project to prove the James Bond theory. I was well prepared for the situation. Despite the known tropical climate of the Puerto Rico, I had brought with me a suit and tie for this occasion. I alone was admitted to the casino and Will returned to his room.

I had never been in a casino before. It was a strange but exciting place. The lights were so low that the room was in semi-darkness and was weirdly quiet considering the number of people present. There were many tables for different types of gambling. I was only interested in the blackjack tables, of which there were about ten. I peeked at several tables and quickly discovered that each table had a pre-determined minimum bet. Some were a hundred dollars and some were ten. I looked for the lowest, and found one table with a minimum bet of only one dollar.

The crucial part was my learning how to play the game. The only blackjack I knew was kid's play; a player made twenty-one and won. It seemed simple enough. I

8

stood by the table and scrutinized everyone's moves. The dealer distributed two cards to each player face up, and then he gave himself two cards with one facedown and one faceup. If a player's hand counted twenty-one, he won. Otherwise the player had a choice of requesting another card or maintaining the current hand. To signal a choice, each player tapped his cards with a finger or hid his cards with a hand. Tapping meant a request of one more card, and hiding was refusal of an additional card. If a player's hand counted more than twenty-one, then the player lost the game. If the player's count was less than twenty-one, then he had another chance to request or refuse an additional card. When nobody wanted more cards, the dealer flipped his facedown card; if his count was less than sixteen, then he was required to add one more card. If the dealer's count exceeded twenty-one, then the remaining players won the game and would receive their payoff. If the dealer's count was higher than the player's count, then the dealer won. If dealer's count was lower than a player's count, then the player won. Payoff was three for two, so when I bet the minimum bet, which was two fifty-cent chips and won, I would get three chips, one dollar fifty cents worth. It seemed there were additional complicated deviations from the basics, but I couldn't understand them. I decided to ignore the complicated parts and to stick to the basics only.

The table was relatively crowded with no vacant player's chair. I stood there and carefully observed the games. Probably ten minutes passed. I noticed that one player's pile of chips was dwindling. I quietly moved behind him. When he ran out of his chips he stood up and left his chair. I quickly moved into his place.

I pulled out a twenty-dollar bill and gave it to the dealer. He gave me forty fifty-cent chips and shoved the bill into a slot on the table with a small plate. It seemed there was a safe or some kind of cash delivery system on the underside of the table. I was curious where the money would go. While I was thinking, the dealer started a new round and was waiting for my signal. I was slightly embarrassed for my absent-mindedness.

My hand was sixteen and his was seven. Bond's scheme said that if the dealer's hand was more than six and your hand was less than seventeen, always request one more card, and otherwise keep the current hand. I tapped my deck, pretending to be a seasoned blackjack player. The new card was the eight of hearts. I lost the round. I lost the next three rounds consecutively. The thought that James Bond's secret scheme might be a fiction flashed in my mind. I reaffirmed to myself that I was a scientist and I had to have faith in mathematical probability. If a player's winning probability were more than half then the player eventually would win in the long run, regardless how small the excess amount of probability over a half was. Nobody could predict win or loss of the outcome of each individual round, but probability would assure the accumulated results of many consecutive games. Wisely Bond's secret scheme also said to stick to the scheme regardless of the outcome of each game or how much loss accumulated. So I determined to myself that I would continuously bet the minimum allowable bet of two chips until I exhausted the supply of my chips. In the fifth game I finally won. It might have been my imagination, but I felt an unfriendly atmosphere at the table, probably due to my monotonous minimum bet for every round. I toughened myself and ignored unfriendly gazes from other players.

After a while, I glanced at my watch. I had already been sitting on the chair for more than two hours! I quickly counted my chips, a total of forty-four. I had gained a total of four chips, two dollars worth, for two hours of continuous playing. At this rate I would never be able to double my money by the morning, I thought. I had to take up a more aggressive betting strategy. There were several betting strategies. Betting strategy didn't change winning probability, but it would change the speed of reaching the goal. A safer strategy was not likely to lose all my resources before reaching the goal, but it would take a longer time than a riskier strategy. I had been using the safest strategy of betting an equal amount every time, regardless of the outcome of the previous round. My estimate of the winning probability of Bond's scheme was about 0.501. Based on the probability and experience of the past two hours, the time required to double my money was more than twenty hours. I needed a better betting strategy.

Aggressive betting strategies would take advantage of a winning streak. If I get a longer winning streak then I accumulate my pot quickly. However, if I have a losing streak, then my pot would diminish quickly. Again the winning probability is the same, so in the long run I would win, but I might lose my entire pot before I had a chance to double the money. I decided to take the second safest betting strategy, namely consecutive increment betting strategy. I would increase my bet by one dollar whenever I won. If I lost a round, then I would return to one dollar. The key to successful use of a betting strategy was to stop betting immediately at the break in the desired length of a winning streak. If I could have a five-game winning streak before running out of my pot, I would be able to double my pot to forty dollars. If I had many losing streaks before the five-game winning streak, then I might exhaust my entire pot.

For both spectators and players, playing with this betting strategy was more interesting, because I would lose more often and quickly. At one point my pot decreased to a mere five chips. However, I recovered quickly, too. Finally I got a five-game winning streak and counted my chips. The total number of chips in my pot was ninety-three, more than double the original forty. I stood up from my chair with my handful of chips and bee-lined it to the cashier. I was exuberant that I finally proved the correctness and practicality of James Bond's secret scheme and I also doubled my money! It was already four o'clock in the morning. I had been playing more than six hours straight. Nevertheless I doubled my money within six hours. How about that! Mathematical theory would never lie. As long as the winning probability was more than half, eventually you would win and you could double or triple your money. The only question was how long it would take to achieve the goal. My experiment showed that an aggressive betting strategy made it possible to double my money within six hours.

As planned, Will and I met at the hotel restaurant for breakfast. Will asked me,

"Yashi, did you double your money last night?"

"Yes, I did, but this morning, rather than last night"

"Then you must buy me breakfast this morning."

"Sure I will, but you must lend me the money."

"Why?"

"Somebody stole my wallet while I was busy doubling my money."

A Night in an Old House

Adam had no idea where he was, but had to keep driving on the narrow twisting dirt road with mountains on his left and a cliff on the right, through drenching rain in the dark of night. He wanted to stop, but he couldn't find any place to pull over in his car. Mud slides or falling rocks might block his way at any moment. Adam was a scientist en route to a remote research station. He had taken a scenic route, instead of the well-mapped recommended route. Thinking he should have stopped at the last motel while it was still light, he saw-ahead an old farm house on a small plateau illuminated by lightning. He pulled up at the side of the house and put on his raincoat. After he banged on the wooden door several times, someone inside said, "Who's there?"

"I lost my way. I'm looking for a place to stay tonight."

A few minutes later, an old man carrying an oil lamp opened the door. After careful inspection, he agreed that Adam could stay just for the night, provided Adam would leave at the earliest possible time the next morning. He hung Adam's dripping raincoat on the peg next to the door, led Adam to the back room, and showed him a bed.

Adam fell asleep as soon as he extinguished the lamp. At first, he thought he was dreaming, then he realized he heard the sound of a young girl giggling. He listened attentively.

"Hi Adam, welcome to my room," the young girl's voice said.

He was startled to see a white glow in the far corner of the room. He tried to light the lamp, but couldn't find a match. He was scared, but she seemed friendly. With his most friendly voice he said, "Hi, Why don't you come closer. I want to talk to you." The only reply he got was a giggle. He asked again, "Who are you, anyway?" This time he got an answer.

"I am Mary and I lived in this room."

Suddenly lightning flashed and temporarily blinded him. When he could see again, the corner of the room was empty. He quickly got up and looked around the hallway. No one was there. He checked inside the room only an empty closet. He went back to bed and eventually dropped off to sleep, dreaming throughout the night. When he woke up in the morning, he was not sure what was a dream and what was real. He found his luggage disturbed. He checked all his belongings, but nothing was missing. When he was ready to leave, the old man and his wife greeted him at the door, but refused to accept his offer of payment.

"We cannot serve you breakfast, but you will find a place about five miles down the road. Bye." The old man opened the door, but he and his wife subtly refused to shake hands with Adam.

There was not a cloud in the sky and the sunshine was strong even in the early morning. When he backed out to the road, he noticed a large tree at the side of the house, probably two hundred years old. To his surprise, it was an elm tree, all of which he believed were killed by Dutch elm disease decades before.

While driving he reviewed the incident of the previous night. He, a scientist, didn't believe in irrational phenomena. Mary was a daughter of the elderly couple, who had a mental illness. Because of the potential embarrassment of her bizarre behavior, they didn't want anyone to see her and wanted Adam to leave their house as soon as possible. That was the explanation.

He stopped at Joe's Coffee Shop for breakfast. Joe, the man behind the counter said, "Did you stay in the Old Elm House the last night?"

"Yes, but how do you know that?" Adam asked.

"No other traveler comes at this time of day," replied Joe and continued, "Did you check all your belongings?"

"Sure, but why? Do they steal things?"

"Not exactly, but Mary does make mischief, collecting small items from young men like you."

"Who is Mary? Is she the daughter of the couple?"

"Yes. Are you sure you have all your belongings? Think hard," Joe emphasized.

Adam thought about it. "Oh, my raincoat was hung near the door. I forgot it."

"It was Mary, OK. Well, it's better to forget the raincoat. It's gone, farewell, adios, bye-bye, sayonara."

"Why is that?"

"Mary died in 1873."

"Are you kidding me?"

"No, Mary had a fiancé who went to the Civil War but didn't come back. She lived with the parents in that house for her whole life and waited and waited for him. She eventually had a mental breakdown and died, then her parents a few years later. The house stood empty for a while until a mysterious fire burned it down in 1923, exactly fifty years after her death. Soon after the fire, a rumor started that the house sometimes appeared to lure a young man."

Adam knew these country folks had lots of tall tales for city visitors. He drove back almost ten miles to retrieve his raincoat, but he couldn't find the Old Elm House. He turned around again and checked all possible sites for a house, in case it was recessed from the road and maybe he missed it the first time. He found only one spot, a small plateau large enough for a house. Shoulder high weeds and thick bushes covered the place. He stopped his car and walked all over. He found the rotten stump of a big tree and three tombstones, barely standing. One of the stone markers said, "Mary Elm, 1845-1873". Adam noticed something beneath the heavily inclined marker. He lifted the stone. It was his raincoat, neatly folded and still damp. He murmured, "There must be a rational explanation."

An International Conference

An elegantly dressed lady came up to me and asked in English, "You are one of the Americans from the Conference, aren't you?"

It happened in the summer of 1969, in the city of Chania, on the island of Crete, Greece. I went there as an American delegate to The First International Space Science and Engineering Conference in Greece, the strangest international conference I have ever participated in. While the local inhabitants were taking their siesta, I took a short walk. I was heading away from the conference hall, a barn-like local movie theater.

There was no traffic, vehicular or pedestrian. The time was early afternoon. The sky was cloudless and the sun strong. The air was hot, but a sea breeze made me comfortable. I could see blue sea to the right and green hills to the left. I was enjoying the tranquility while contemplating the events of the past three days. She interrupted my thinking, but I quickly regained my composure and answered, "Yes, I am."

"I was impressed by your presentation," she said.

I was really surprised. It was an engineering conference at which women attendants were rare, even in the States. I asked her, "Are you an engineer?"

"No, but I attended all the sessions to listen to English."

"Are you a school teacher?

"No, I used to be a school teacher, but I now teach English privately."

That was understandable. The official language of the conference was English, even though most of the conference speakers were Greek, Cypriot, and other Greek-speaking people. It had to be the greatest opportunity for anyone who wanted to learn English, because English-speaking tourists are unlikely to visit the city. It has no attractions, accommodations, or transportation for tourists.

I had noticed that about a hundred or more people attended every session, despite there were only fifty conference participants. Most of the audience were from the local high school and sat on folding chairs in the rear half of the hall. They had to be coming to listen to English, too.

She asked, "Would you come to my home?"

I was delighted with her request and raised my illicit hope. I heard that Greek ladies were aggressive, but so quick and straight! How old is she? She is not beautiful but attractive. "Oh, yes, of course," I said and added "but why?"

"I want you to talk to my students. They need to practice their English."

Her statements were a big disappointment for me. So I said, "Why me? As you see, I am not a born American and English is not my native tongue. There are several other American delegates in this conference. You should ask those Americans who speak real English."

"I asked every one of them, but none of them accepted my plea. Please come to my home and speak to my students. They have been waiting for an American every day for the past three days. Please, come to my house. You seem to be a very kind person. I desperately need an American who will talk to my students. I promised them I'd bring an American today. If I don't, they will be tremendously disappointed. They probably will never again have chance to speak to an American at all. Foreign visitors never come to this city."

I thought, "Oh, boy. I am getting into trouble. I have to give English conversation lessons to a bunch of Greek students. I have a hard time myself to speak English. I am putting myself in an embarrassing position. I never met this lady until this moment. Why do I have to do anything for her? All other Americans refused her request, so can I."

While I was thinking, she continued. "Please, please, come and talk to my students."

I was still thinking, "What do I lose? Even if I have to embarrass myself, so what? Nobody knows me here and we will never meet again. She is asking me: a Japanese-turned-American, who speaks with heavily-accented English. She must be really desperate. I have no specific plan for this afternoon, anyway. Why don't I help her? It may turn out to be a good thing. Who knows?" I finally said to her, "OK. If you think I can do the job, then I will go with you."

After walking together for about fifteen minutes, we reached a residential section of the city. A thick stone wall surrounded every house. The wall was so high that even the tallest person couldn't peek inside. I wondered what the inside looked like. She led me into one of those houses.

Inside of the stone wall, there was a small courtyard. It was much cooler, compared to outside, because of the shade from trees and walls. A small table and chairs were set up in the courtyard. Two students were waiting for us. She introduced me to them and we started talking in English. One of the students was twenty-eight years old and wanted to migrate to the States in the future. The other was eight years old. Both were the most advanced students from her class. They had never practiced their English with anyone else from outside of their class. They were so eager to find out so many things:

"What do real Americans do?"

"What does the real America look like?"

"How good is our English?"

We practiced our English for about two hours. In my opinion, their English was very good. I was a little sorry for them, since they could not get a "real" American. Well, better than nothing. I did my best and it seemed they enjoyed it, too.

When I had to say good-bye, she gave me a small package as a token of her thanks. She said that I should not open the package until I was home. It was mysterious, but I promised her that I would not open it until then.

During supper that evening, I confided my adventure to John, one of the American delegates. He was a professor from University of Gettysburg, or some place which I never heard of. He said that I was lucky. He had been trying to practice his Greek with local people, but the Greek government had provided our guide-interpreter Prof. Pappas, who interfered each time. John thought Prof. Pappas was a spy from the Greek Secret Service whose job was to prevent us from making contact with local people.

I asked him, "Why do the Greeks want to prevent us making contact?"

"Don't you know that Chania was the center of the armed opposition to the current government, which took over the previous government by a *coup d'état*? Don't you know the reason why the Greek government held this ludicrous conference in this remote city and paid all expenses for international delegates, even providing the special charter flight from Athens that carried all conference participants here?"

"No, I don't. I have no idea," I replied.

"Because the government wants to show the world, or more specifically the United States, that there is no more armed rebellion and Greece is a stable country," he said.

"Now I know why His Excellency, Regent General Nikolandamus himself came to this conference opening ceremony."

"Yes, he came with bodyguards who were more numerous than the entire conference's participants," John added.

"Then why did they have to watch us?" I asked.

"Because they are afraid that rebels might contact us to tell the true situation. So they sent Professor Pappas to watch us. But you hang around with Japanese delegates more often than with us, so they thought you were safe and overlooked the possibility you would make the contact with local people," he concluded.

When I came back from supper, I noticed the Japanese book on my desk was upside down. It seemed that someone who couldn't read Japanese had disturbed my book. I checked my belongings, but nothing was missing. I had, however, a nagging feeling that the souvenir which I received from the lady was different, from what was now on my desk.

A few days later, when I came home I opened the souvenir. It was a cheap ceramic plaque with Greek mythological images. I thought it cheap, because the picture of gods was only on the left side of the plaque and the right side was blank. It looked like a factory reject. Nevertheless, I hung the plaque on my wall. Whenever I look at it, I wonder whether it was the real souvenir she gave me, or not. If it was real, then why did she say I was no to open it until I arrived home. Or has the imperfect image some meaning? I will never know. It was just a memento from the strange conference.

Part Three
In Traditional Industry

A 2000 Pound Word Processor

It was before Bill Gates and before WordPerfect. It was the middle of 1970s. My employer decided to market a word processor, called Wordplex system, consisted of four desk-size units: a central processor, two disk drive storage units (one for main and the other for backup), and a tape drive unit. Each storage unit could store 10,000 pages of documents. If we use the tape unit, we could expand its storage capacity to the infinite by shifting data from the disk to tapes. The total system, of which price was $200,000 weighed more than 2000 pounds and occupied a medium-size office room.

One day, a group of customers from Detroit visited our demonstration room. They expressed a keen interest in our word processor system. Joe, the head of our marketing, let the leader of the group sit at the control console, not at a typing station, the usual seat for customers. I, as head of technical staff, indicated disapproval on this move by shaking my head. This could be an invitation to disaster! Just like yielding pilot's seat to a passenger. Joe winked at me as a signal of, "Don't worry. I know what I am doing."

The leader emanated confidence. As soon as he sat on the chair, he typed something. The console screen showed fast moving rows of numbers. If he was surprised, he didn't show it and pressed another key. The console screen went to blank. He said, "Did I do something wrong?" Joe said, "No, this system is indestructible. Don't worry, Yashi will put back the system in no time."

I said, "Well, I have to restart the system. It will take about 5 minutes." When I restarted system, the console screen reported, "No main storage unit available." I was in a panic. It was the major disaster which we had never experienced. I shut down the system and whispered to Joe. "Hey, Joe. We lost the main storage unit. We have to terminate this demo."

"No, you cannot do that. This is our first real prospect. If we quit here, we lose our chance. I understand that the backup and the main are identical units. So use the backup and restart the system."

"Joe, you don't understand. Yes, we can do that theoretically. But then we will not be able to retrieve a document from the new main storage. The purpose of the backup is to restore data into the system when the system is running with a new blank main storage. The backup was not designed for the direct retrieval of documents."

"I don't care how you do it, but you have to restart the system and let me do all talking. OK?" I reluctantly agreed with him and reconnected the backup as a main storage unit.

Joe approached the executive, "Alex, we discovered that a system file was modified and we lost connection to the main storage unit. I thought it was a god-send opportunity to show you how easily we could restore the system when we lost the main storage." Joe explained the party, "We disconnected the main storage unit and reconnected a backup unit in place of the main unit. Yashi, start the system."

After a few minutes, the console screen displayed a message "System ready." Joe said, "See? This demonstrates that even when we had damaged a main storage unit, we could restore the system within ten minutes."

One of the men asked, "Can we see a document now?"

"O, sure. Yashi, retrieve a document," Joe confidently ordered me. I had been afraid of that kind of request. If I issue the normal document retrieval commands, the system would respond, "Main storage is not accessible." I had to think fast. I quickly typed commands in such a way that no one could see what these were. The screen showed the document. Joe said," See this is the document which we saw before."

I knew it was not the document they saw before. Many of our documents looked similar, so a glance wouldn't tell the difference between one document and another. In contrast to Joe's apparent confidence, I felt uneasy and nervous. Joe continued. "Since it's almost lunch time, we should go to lunch and continue our demonstration after lunch, if you wish." They left.

Later I asked Joe, "You seemed so confident that time. Did you really believe I could retrieve a document from the backup storage unit?"

"No, I knew it was impossible. But a part of my job is showing confidence under any circumstance. In reality, I was sweating under my arms. Then to my surprised, you pulled out a rabbit from the hat. How did you do it?"

"That is a part of my job," I said.

Only a few weeks after the incident, Wang Laboratories announced a revolutionary word processor with a price tag of a mere 30,000 dollars. Within three months of this announcement, we had to close down our word processor division before we made even a single sale.

A quarter century later, I wrote this article with my word processor. It costs less than 1000 dollar, weighs twenty pounds, but produces a better quality document with a faster speed than my yesteryear's 200,000 dollar, 2000 pound word processor did.

Jack, the MBA

"Yashi, we are on the road to becoming millionaires," Jack said.

"How?" I replied with the thought that Jack was joking again.

"I have an order for forty-eight thousand new copiers."

"Wow, that is a really big order! Indeed, that might put us on the road to becoming millionaires, but..." I hesitated.

"What do you mean 'But...' It's a sure thing! The customer was Davidson Machine Company, one of the giants of the copier business."

It was in the early nineteen-seventies when the basic patent of the Xerox process expired and my company, ECI, entered the lucrative office copier business. My new Xerox-type copier, ECI-20, with a speed of twenty copies-per-minute (20 CPM) was an engineering masterpiece which could become a best seller in the small business market. The only problem was that ECI didn't have the necessary sales and distribution network. So I had brought Jack, a young and ambitious MBA, into my company as a business partner.

Jack was remarkable; he established a marketing department and organized a distribution network for the new copier. I was glad to see the change but sometimes I felt it was too fast for me. For instance, how could we produce two thousand machines every month, as the Davidson order would require, considering that our existing production capacity was one hundred machines per month? ECI had no resources to expand existing production capacity even a little bit. When I mentioned my concern to Jack, he said, "Yashi! Don't worry, I will take care of it."

To my surprise, Jack found a financial backer for the expansion, a Japanese trading company. Mitsutomo & Co., agreed, but with a price: a minority ownership of ECI, and a commission payment for every machine shipped from the new production facility.

For a while, our road to becoming millionaires seemed to be smoothly paved. Then I noticed a rapidly increasing number of replacements in the drum, the key component of the copier. I found that the quality of the drums had deteriorated since the expansion of our manufacturing capacity. Engineers had been working day and night to solve the problem, but unsuccessfully as yet.

I wanted an immediate suspension of copier shipments and recall of all copiers from the field. Jack objected to my wishes and said that stopping shipment and recalling copiers would be suicide for ECI. He believed that there would be enough time to resolve the drum problem before a majority of customers, including Davidson, would notice the problem. So shipment of the copying machines with inferior drums continued.

Unbeknownst to us, Davidson had their own secret. Davidson's business had been in the leasing of high-speed copiers to major industrial companies. Their machines were based on special copying paper, which only Davidson could produce. It was a profitable business, but its customer base started to erode gradually as the cost of Xerox copying came down.

Facing this crisis, Davidson brought new blood, their own young and ambitious MBA's, into their top management. Those new managers wanted to replace their old-fashioned copiers with new Xerox-type ones, purchased from a small company, which Davidson could manipulate with their vast financial resources. They chose our ECI-20. Test marketing to the small business market under its own brand name, DMC-20, went well.

When Davidson tried to place DMC-20's with their major leasing customers, those customers refused to replace their old fashioned 40 CPM machines with the new slower DMC-20 machines. Davidson needed a Xerox-type and faster (40 CPM) copier to replace existing machines to prevent the defection of those customers to competitors. The company solved this problem with a clever trick. Davidson's engineers discovered that our ECI-20 could be upgraded to a 40 CPM machine, called DMC-40, by simply speeding up paper feed. The conversion process was so simple that a serviceman could perform it during installation at customer sites. So Davidson decided to deliver DMC-40's to its existing customers. They didn't tell us about the converted machine.

These two secrets in both companies collided and surfaced as numerous customer complaints. The thing we knew but Davidson didn't was the fact that the useful drum life is determined by a complex function of the copying speed. For instance, doubling the copying speed would reduce the life span of the copier to one-eighth. Because of that, I had carefully chosen the copying speed of 20 CPM for ECI-20 by balancing customer desire for a faster speed with a consideration of drum replacement cost. Davidson broke the balance by doubling the copying speed.

As a result, the drum life of the DMC-40 was extremely short compared to the original life span of the ECI-20. In addition, the inferior quality drum cut the shortened life expectancy further.

As soon as the first DMC-40 was placed at a customer site, customer complaints started to come in. The quantity of complaints rapidly increased as the number of delivered machines grew. All complaints were similar: the print quality of the new copiers deteriorated badly on the second day and the drums had to be replaced within a week.

Facing this serious situation, Davidson's management called an emergency meeting with us to discuss possible solutions for those complaints. The meeting was a mess; we screamed, yelled and blamed each other for our own problems. Eventually the coolness of the MBA's prevailed and we generated plans for remedial actions:

ECI would put more effort into a resolution of the drum-manufacturing problem and complete, as quickly as possible, the development of ECI-40, a faster machine with a new type of drum. Meanwhile shipments of ECI-20 to Davidson would be cut to half. Davidson would concentrate on selling DMC-20's to the small business market; terminate activities related to DMC-40, and wait for the new ECI-40.

Within two months of the meeting, we solved the drum production problem and completed the development of the ECI-40 copier. Jack again started saying, "We are on the road to becoming millionaires."

Only one month after the debut of the ECI-40, The Wall Street Journal printed an article about Davidson withdrawing from the copier business completely to concentrate on a computer application business, and also filing a suit against ECI for breach of contract.

I was shocked and upset not only by the contents of the article, but also by how I found out about the change-- not directly from Davidson management, but from a newspaper. I felt like the ground was cracked open under me and formed a big sinkhole that swallowed me up. Contrary to my reaction, Jack was cool and said to me, "Yashi! These things are part of the business world. Don't worry, I will take care of it."

First, Jack reached an out-of-court settlement with Davidson with the help of a legal team from Mitsutomo and then he filed a bankruptcy for ECI. Both Jack and I were forced to resign. Mitsutomo took over most of the assets of ECI and then sold it to Canpson, a major copier company. It was no surprise to me when Canpson selected Jack to run the division. Soon people heard Jack saying again, "We are on the road to becoming millionaires."

Once I had realized that Jack's "we" didn't include me, I immediately retired and moved to South Florida. Nowadays I am enjoying warm weather, despite the potential danger of the opening up of a new sinkhole in my back yard, similar to the one that I fell into on the way to becoming a millionaire.

Pirate's Treasure

"**I** have a coded document which might be worth millions of dollars. Can you decipher it for me?" a stranger asked me in the company cafeteria.

"I do cryptography as a hobby but I'm not professional. How do you know my hobby? I never told anyone about it. And who are you?"

"I am Walter Russell, a temp working in the Components Section. Several months ago, you won a prize in the contest in Transmission Engineers magazine by solving a puzzle called 'UFO's message', didn't you? I thought anyone who could decode that message could do this job, too. I got this temporary assignment to this company so I could approach you."

"In this business, there are so many mine fields. I am not interested in anything related to espionage or national security."

"Don't worry. It's an antique document. Naturally I will pay you."

Next day he brought a facsimile of the document, which consisted of several sheets of blue paper on which blue letters were printed. They were hard to read. I asked, "I know that you don't want me to have the original document, but can you make a better copy, like normal black letters on white paper?"

"No and I don't want you to make any copies of this document. This is a copier-proof special document which nobody can copy," he replied.

The document contained hand written letters of probably the English alphabet with some accent marks like French and no spacing or punctuation. There was no obvious pattern I could recognize. I said, "It seems like a tough one. It might take a long time for me to figure it out. I need background information and the circumstances by which you got the document."

"Can you decipher it without background information?"

"Yes, but with lots of wasted effort and sidetracking on my part. I would also like to make sure I am not entangled with national security."

Reluctantly he told me the document was a part of a secret map, passed down through several generations of an old mariner's family in Freeport, Massachusetts. According to legend, the map described the details of a treasure buried by Handless the Pirate, who ravaged the northeastern coast of the United States in the seventeenth century. He was notorious because he cut off the hand of any opponents or uncooperative victims. He collected only gold and silver, ignoring jewelry and other valuables. He successfully operated for several decades but never got caught. His identity was still a mystery today.

"How much is the buried treasure worth?" I asked.

"It is estimated at 400 million dollars in the current gold market."

"How much will you pay me?"

"Ten thousand dollars for a full translation." That was lots of money then, about six months of my salary. "And," he added, "If you finish it within one month, I will give you another ten thousand as a bonus."

I immediately accepted the job. At first I analyzed the document with standard technique using a computer and commercial deciphering programs to speed it up. My thinking was that the pirate might be well educated by standards of the time, but he was not familiar with modern cryptography, so the code could be broken with standard methods. However, he also was aware of the fact that a potential decoder would be familiar with all conventional techniques. So the pirate must have incorporated an odd twist or two. My challenge was to find the twist. Eventually, I did find it. Before ciphering the text he rearranged it using a combination of mirror images and inverted images, interweaving every other character. It took me about four weeks.

The deciphered document told how to find the markers. Starting at the island of Nantucket, it went island hopping: one island to the next, then five islands later it pointed out the target island. Once the target island was reached, there was a sequence of several markers, including several false markers to prevent accidental discovery of the real ones. It was a well-thought-out burial plan. Even in the case of a natural disaster which might wash away some markers, the built-in redundancy assured finding the final burial place of the treasure.

Once I finished the translation, I brought it to my office and visited Walter in the Components section. He wasn't there. I asked his supervisor about him. He told me that Walter left the company four weeks ago. I called the number he gave me and left a message on an answering machine.

The very next day I got a call from him and we made a lunch date. During lunch, he checked my translation and seemed satisfied. Then he made a pitch that I should invest my twenty thousand dollars in their enterprise, the digging up of the Handless the Pirate Treasure. If I did so, I would be a full partner with four others, who would receive one-fifth of whatever they recovered. Besides Walter, the other partners were the owner of a salvage and dredging company, who would supply the necessary equipment and manpower; an antique dealer, who would be responsible for converting findings to cash; and a lawyer who would handle ownership issues and fight with the state to maximize our shares.

It was a very tempting offer, with the investment of twenty thousand for a potential return of eight million dollars. But I had a serious reservation: how would I know when and what they will discover? Would they inform me if they recovered the treasure? They would have no incentive to tell me about the discovery. It took a while to reach my final decision. I said no. One bird in the hand was better than two in the bush. I wanted the full twenty thousand as promised. He said that he didn't have enough time to prepare the full amount, so had brought only one thousand dollars. The rest would be ready the following week at the same time and the same place. He also didn't return the translation, despite my protest.

I was naïve enough to go to the restaurant the following week and wait two hours, but he never showed up. A call to his number was answered by a recorded message saying the number was no longer in service. I drove to his address. It was a vacant lot.

I was duped out of nineteen thousand dollars, but I had a small consolation prize. One of the things he didn't know was that the deciphered document was not as precise as he had assumed. Deciphering is not an exact process, especially when only a single document is involved. The resulting translation might include many potential errors and uncertainties; both accidental and intentional. Furthermore, I had included several crucial errors in my translation with the intention of making a separate errata sheet after I was fully paid. I made sure that they would never find the buried treasure unless they paid me in full.

This happened more than a quarter century ago. Later I learned that they had abandoned the project after ten years of effort. I still have the direction to the buried treasure. Does anyone want to buy a pirated copy of a pirate's document? It's cheap, only twenty thousand dollars in cash.

Shoplifters, Be Aware!

My first encounter with shoplifting happened with my sixth grade classmates. Three of us went on an excursion to collect applications from several middle schools. We had an extra allowance for lunch and trolley fares. After visiting the schools we stopped at a big department store. I had never been in a department store before. It was a dazzling and exciting place. We split up and went to different counters. I went to the book department and bought a pocket dictionary which I had wanted for a long time. Sato bought a harmonica and Ume bought something, too. When we asked what he bought, he simply pointed to his pocket. We strolled out of the store. A middle-aged man with a fedora stopped us just a few steps away. He said that he worked for the store and wanted to see our receipts. He casually inspected Sato's and mine, but really scrutinized Ume's. He said that the receipt didn't agree with his purchased item, which turned out to be a small pencil sharpener. Ume had to go back to the store with him, but we could go home. We were surprised at this development, but we realized we couldn't go home without Ume. We went back into the store. We couldn't find them, even though we went up and down the stairs of all five floors looking for them. Eventually the closing bell rang and we were forced to leave. We reluctantly went home.

When I arrived, it was dark. My parents were worried about me. They questioned me about where I had been, why I was late, etc. I hesitated to betray my friend by revealing the truth. When they heard my story, they got excited. They were convinced I had told the truth, and my father contacted my school next day. My teacher confirmed my story with Sato and probably from Ume's confession. I was ashamed and felt guilty for putting Ume in an embarrassing position. I asked him what had happened after he was taken back into the store. He said that they went to one of the back offices and he answered a few questions like his name, address, school, etc. Then they released him. His lack of shame and remorse astonished me. We went separate ways from that point on. I understood that the only punishment he suffered was that our teacher refused to write a good recommendation letter.

A few decades later, fate led me to selling shoplifting prevention devices to big retail chains like Sears. The basic principle of these devices was simple. We embedded a small active marker into the merchandise. When a customer purchased the merchandise, the cashier would deactivate or remove the marker so that when the merchandise left the store with the customer, the detector at the store exit wouldn't be triggered.

I knew of a Savage (not the real name) discount chain store located in central Pennsylvania, one of our best customers. Their store was a model of shoplift-proofing. The manager told me that the store had suffered tremendous losses from shoplifting under the previous management and was on the brink of closure. When he took it on he remodeled it and installed high tech shoplift prevention and detection devices. The major changes in remodeling were to widen the aisles for easy surveillance and to narrow the cashier's lanes, the entrance and one exit. The narrowness, combined with intentional corners, made quick-in-and-out traffic difficult and the installation of an effective shoplifting detection system easier. The store also had both real and decoy security cameras and two-way mirrors. According to him, despite these high-tech gadgets, the most effective deterrent was the store policy of zero-tolerance prosecution of shoplifters. Big notices of the policy were posted all over. He literally meant zero-tolerance and practiced it. A shoplifter who stole even something as small as a lipstick was arrested, sent to the police station, and prosecuted. Shoplifting decreased to almost zero, profit increased, and the store prospered. To our great disappointment, the chain was reluctant to adopt the same system chain-wide.

Fortunately we found another good customer, the Amicable (not its real name) chain. Each Amicable store bought as much of our equipment as the Savage model store. A new Amicable opened within a few blocks of the model Savage store. The Amicable store was completely different from Savage. It had a wide open entrance so that shoppers would feel welcomed. Surprisingly, within a year or so the Savage store went out of business. There are many reasons for a store to succeed or to fail. That is the nature of the business. I was curious about the struggle between these two stores from the viewpoint of shoplifting prevention since they took opposite attitudes toward shoplifters. I secured an appointment from the busy store manager of the Amicable store.

His opening statement in our interview almost dropped me out of my chair. He said that he encouraged casual shoplifting. He bought many shoplift prevention systems, but these were not to catch thieves. He wanted to know what merchandise they were stealing and who was doing it. Shoplifting was one of the best market research tools he had. The most difficult part of retail business was to know what merchandise customers want to buy. He tracked almost all shoplifters using high tech devices. Naturally he arrested and prosecuted all professionals and high-ticket item shoplifters. He paid special attention to young shoplifters, because young people were the largest customer group. He selectively caught them and took action to prevent escalation and mass shoplifting. In his opinion, the Savage store had prospered only because there was no competition. Once a new welcoming Amicable store opened with similar discount prices, customers flocked to the friendly store. He warned me that if I was a celebrity or any notable person, I had to watch myself. It was too good an opportunity for a store to miss out on great advertisement. Shoplifting was a public endorsement of the store, showing that the store was good enough for the famous person to shop there. He concluded his remarks, "We are in the business of selling merchandise to people, not to protect merchandise from people."

Temporary Permanence

I was hesitant to hire a temp but there was no choice. Temps were expensive, their capabilities questionable and their work attitude unreliable. I was in charge of developing a new product that would overturn competitors and revitalize the company. I had one electronic technician, Steve. I needed three of them to finish my project, but the company had imposed a hiring freeze. It was the middle of the eighties.

George was recommended for this project by an old friend, who said, "Trust me, you will not regret hiring George."

I interviewed George, "What is your experience?"

"I built micro-computers to control different machinery. I designed, assembled, and tested by myself, nothing else."

"What school did you go to?" I questioned.

"I graduated high school, that's all. All electronic skills are self taught."

"How long do you intend to stay with us?"

"As long as you need me, but I would like to participate from the beginning to the end of a new product development cycle. I am the best technician for new product development and I want to maintain that position."

"Whoa, that's a big claim. Up front, I have to tell you, you may be the best technician in the world, but I can offer you only a temp position now. If it works out, then I may offer you a permanent position."

"Thank you, but I will never accept a permanent position. I want to work as a temp and get paid accordingly," George replied.

"How come?" I asked. I couldn't imagine anyone refusing an employment opportunity in our company, one of the Fortune Five Hundred companies with 150 years' history.

"A permanent employee pay scale is too low. As a temp, I will work like hell and collect as much pay as I can. In addition, no single company has enough new product development projects. The product development cycle will be shortened from the current two years to six months within the next five years. I want to be involved in this fast moving field. If I was employed by a big company, I would miss exciting opportunities," George answered.

I was stunned at his frankness. At that time, the pay scale for a temp was about three times that of a comparable regular employee. I hired him for three months as a test period. Once I was pleased with his performance, I extended his contract to the duration of my project.

During working hours he was stoic and never wasted company time. His work was methodical and meticulous. The only thing I didn't like was that he refused to do any paper work or any non-essential work. He insisted that if he did such work, he would not complete his project within the promised time. To complete the project in time, I honored his request and routed his paper work to someone else.

Steve, my first technician, had a bachelor's degree in electronics, but his technical capability was so-so. He was a second-generation employee and had good connections in the company. His father still worked in another department. He had more clout than I. He was friendly and loved to chat with anyone. Since he had many acquaintances who knew him since babyhood, he chatted with every visitor to our lab and wasted his work hours.

Because of good results with George, I hired another temp. I was willing to pay top price, the same as for George. I got John who had an associate degree in electronics. His experience and skill were comparable to George's. John had the ambition of early retirement like George. John was amicable and accepted any assignment, including the quantity of paper work the Engineering department produced; schematic drawings, wiring diagrams, timing charts, parts lists, compliance reports, etc. His biggest fault was his inability to talk while he was working. Since he and Steve shared the same lab, they wasted lots of time chatting.

George never joined the chitchat. Even when he had to join some conversations, his hands never stopped and his eyes were focused on his work. I thought if I had only George and John, my project might have been in better shape.

One day, Steve informed me that he would be transferred to another project team. I knew that his transfer required my approval as well as that of the supervisor of the other project. Since Steve had many connections in the company, I had no way to veto his move. Instead I used his transfer to my advantage. I told my boss I could finish my project in time with two technicians, provided departmental secretaries handled our paper work. Since a secretary's pay was much lower than a technician, he approved. Steve's self-initiated transfer improved our working conditions and my project moved at a faster pace. I became optimistic that we could finish the project within the preset goal.

A few weeks later, the busiest times for my project, John announced he was taking a higher paying job in another company. I resented his move, but I didn't say anything. As a temp, he could come and go any time he wanted. I could have offered better pay, but why should I pay him more than George who did a much better job?

I had to hire another temp, Jim, who was less experienced. He received less pay than John. Fortunately Jim was a hard worker. Three months later, John wanted to come back to my project, but I refused. How could I rely on him after he had left my project when I needed him most? With the help of George and Jim and with lots of overtime payment, I completed my project in time and within budget. We had developed the world's fastest custom price-tag generator. In-time in-budget completion was rare in new product development projects. Because of this success, I received the "Best New Product Development Manager" award.

When I asked George if he wanted to work on my next project, he said that he wanted to expand his experience and left our company. This was my first experience with the new generation of temp workers, who don't rely on a secure job with a big company. Within two years, a competitor purchased my employer. As a result, everyone, including, Steve and myself, was unemployed.

Last time I heard, George had retired in Florida at age thirty-nine and was raising horses and breeding dogs.

Diamond Trouble

"Half of all diamonds in the market are fake." So a magazine article declared. It was the early nineteen-nineties when low-cost diamonds started flooding the market. The article said that experienced persons or conventional diamond testers could easily distinguish real diamonds from cubic zirconia and other traditional fakes. However there were new simulated diamonds, moissanite, made of synthetic silicon carbide (SiC), with characteristics similar to real diamonds in almost every aspect except cost — less than one-tenth of real ones. Even trained gemologists have to use special equipment in a laboratory set up to separate the simulated from the genuine. If the moissanite was already set in jewelry, even professionals couldn't identify it.

I read the article while I was working in a small electronics company as a new-product development engineer. I decided to invent a diamond detector which could distinguish real diamonds from the moissanite. I believed every jewelry store in the world would buy the detector, then our company could make a bundle.

A diamond has several unique characteristics which no other materials have. The most well-known is its hardness. The diamond is the hardest material in the universe, but moissanite is the second hardest. Its brilliance, called the refraction index, is high, but the simulated one is too. A lesser-known but useful characteristic is its thermal conductivity. A diamond transmits heat better than any other material excluding moissanite. Existing diamond testers use the difference in heat transmission to separate the real stone from traditional imitations, but couldn't separate moissanite because the difference in thermal conductivity is very small. I thought that the difference of heat transmission existed, however small it was. A sophisticated computer program could separate one from the other. So I should be able to make a diamond detector by incorporating a smart computer into a conventional diamond tester.

The basic principle of a diamond tester was simple. A small heater would touch the surface of the diamond first, then a sensor would immediately measure its temperature. In my detector, a thumbnail size micro-chip computer would process the temperature data and separate the bona fide diamond from the simulated stone.

I built a prototype diamond detector which consisted of a pen-like probe and a brick-size display box. The probe contained a heater and a sensor head; the box housed a meter, a micro-chip computer and other control circuits. I spent most of my development effort making the correct computer program to distinguish real diamonds from the moissanite. I had to make lots of assumptions about characteristics based on information available in scientific literature, since I had no physical specimens, diamond or moissanite.

When I completed the detector, I needed to confirm its functionality with real diamond and moissanite. For instance, a larger moissanite might behave like a small real diamond, or vice versa. Also moissanite set on a gold ring might act like an unset true diamond, since the gold might interfere with the cooling of the stone. These nitty-gritty details had to be settled by using specimens of genuine diamond and authentic moissanite.

I thought everybody would welcome the detector. I called a local jeweler and asked his cooperation to calibrate my detector. He flatly refused. He said that such an instrument would undercut the authority and integrity of gemologists, so the instrument would do more harm than good. It was a disheartening reaction, but I had to keep going.

I decided to buy a real diamond and test the instrument with it. I took my wife to the Azul Jewelry store in the mall. I bought a quarter carat diamond ring for $500 for my wife. When I asked for assurance of the authenticity of the diamond, the store clerk said it was real and handed us a certificate, a standard printed form. Next day I brought the ring to my office and tested it with my instrument. It was bogus, a cubic zirconia, not even a simulated diamond. I called my wife and told her.

"Oh, no. What will you do?" she said.

"I will bring the ring back to the store and exchange it for a real one." I went back to the store and argued. They didn't acknowledge that it was fake and refused to exchange it. The best I could get was a full refund. Next I went to my boss and requested funding for purchase of a real diamond and moissanite for the purpose of the detector calibration. Instead of giving me the fund, he suggested that I borrow a diamond from the company president. His wife was famous for her big diamond ring, probably five carats or so. When I explained my problem to the president, he agreed to ask his wife to let her diamond be used to calibrate my diamond detector.

The very next day, I heard a woman's loud voice saying, "Who is Yashi?"

I jumped up from my chair, met her in the hallway and invited her to my office. It was the wife of the company president. I immediately recognized her even though I had never met her before. She had the ring with a big diamond on her right middle finger.

When I asked to borrow it, she said, "Idiot, do you think I will take this ring off for you?"

I brought in my instrument from the lab and set it up on my desk. When I asked her to place her hand on the desk, she hesitated, so I quickly pulled out several tissues and wiped the desk surface clean. Then she reluctantly placed her hand on the desk. I pulled out the sensor pen of my instrument and pressed its tip to a flat surface of the diamond. The tip of my probe was a small sphere just like a ballpoint pen. I kept the probe there about one second. The meter needle indicated the number nine. The meter had a full scale of ten. Theoretically a real diamond should always point at ten, and a good simulated diamond, namely the moissanite, eight. The zone between eight and ten was a gray area in which the dividing line between true and simulated ones existed. The purpose of the calibration was to determine the location of the line. When she saw the meter needle, her color went pale, then red.

She said, "What does this mean?"

I said, "Well, the meter couldn't determine whether it is a genuine diamond or a simulated one, but please don't worry about the reading. I couldn't set the instrument properly since we didn't have…"

"What do you mean don't worry," she interrupted my explanation. "This gadget is junk. You've wasted my time." She quickly left the room.

The same afternoon, my boss called me and said, "Yashi, I am sorry to say, our new reorganization plan has eliminated your position, effective immediately. We will mail your severance pay and personal belongings later. Now security will escort you to the gate."

Sand Bars

It was a day of celebration and the saddest day of my career. I had completed the difficult installation of our new automation system in the main distribution center of X-Mart, a major retail chain. I had been working day and night for three months on site as special project manager. In exchange for the good news of my project completion, the home office sent me the bad news: a competitor bought out our company and my job was eliminated.

After we signed the necessary paperwork, I said to Fran, my counterpart in X-Mart, "You are lucky to have a secure job. For a while, I thought my job was secure, too. Now I have to start looking around. Finding a new job is not easy when I am fifty-five years old."

She replied, "You are referring to the influence of my husband. Sure, he is the vice president of X-mart, but I can do my job without his help. People don't think that way. They see me as a dummy sitting at this position because of my husband. Since you are the best manager I know, I will give you some advice. Do you sail?"

"No, I don't sail."

"Both my husband and I do. If you go sailing, you occasionally hit a sand bar. These sand bars move every day and are not listed on charts. When men face a crisis, they panic and take the attitude of "fight or flight." Men don't know it, but there is another way; keep calm, assess the situation and figure out other options. This is women's thing. If you have small children with you, you cannot choose only fight or flight. Women always try to find another option. When you hit a sand bar, a wrong move will make the situation worse and might sink the boat. Keep calm and carefully assess the tide, wind, time of the day, traffic of other boats, etc. Sometimes the best move is to do nothing and wait only a couple of hours for the rising tide. A career is like a sailing boat. It occasionally hits a sand bar. Even in my husband's position, there is no security. Your career boat just hit a sand bar. Keep calm and evaluate your options. Good luck in your job search. I will be glad to be your reference."

That happened seventeen years ago. I got a job in a high tech company because I took her advice and applied for a project manger's job rather than an engineering position. For ten more years, I survived in the corporate life, finally retiring to Florida when I became sixty-five.

One day I was shopping in a local Y-Mart chain store, I met Fran. We got caught up with each other's lives for a while.

"Our career boat hit a sand bar when Y-Mart bought out X-Mart," she told me. "My husband and I were fired. I had prepared for that. We moved to Florida and bought a house in Del Ray Beach."

At first everything went well, but her husband got restless. He tried to find a job haphazardly but never found any. He started to drink heavily and invested in various quick-buck schemes. Their savings dwindled and their life disintegrated. He became an alcoholic and spent his time on their sailboat. She took a job as a yacht broker to support the family since her husband contributed nothing to household expenses. Three years ago, she decided to divorce him because she had two young boys to bring up. Her husband begged her to give him one more chance. He said that he had a sure way to make enough money, with which they could restore their former life style forever. She didn't know the details, but he said it was about real estate in the Bahamas and nothing illegal. He borrowed as much money as he could, even taking a second mortgage on their house and sailed to the Bahamas saying he would come back within thirty days. That was the last time she ever heard from him.

After two months, she filed a missing person report. A few months later she got a notice from U.S. Coast Guard saying that his sailboat had been found on a sand bar off a small uninhabited island of the Bahamas. There was no sign of anyone on board. As far as the Coast Guard and Bahamian police could determine, there was no trace of any foul play. The boat was still floating but heavily damaged, not from weather but from vandalism. Everything of any value was stripped. The boat had to be scrapped.

Using her connections as a yacht broker, she intensified her effort to collect information about her husband. There were rumors flying around that he was involved in a drug deal. He had left the boat in the Bahamas and flew to Colombia. When he returned, he withdrew all his money from a Bahamian bank and hid the cash somewhere, either on an uninhabited island or on his boat. At least one person had heard him boasting that he hid the money so well nobody could find it without his help. Then he sailed to an unknown destination. From that time on, he simply disappeared from the surface of the earth. One contact believed that he was betrayed by a drug dealer or that local thugs captured him to get his money. Since the boat was floating when it was found, the bandits probably believed the money was hidden there and ransacked it. They seemingly never found the money. If they had found it, they would have sunk the boat. When the Coast Guard discovered the boat, the thugs likely killed him and dumped his body in the sea for barracuda food.

The rumors of the murder of her husband didn't help Fran. Her husband was missing, not dead from the legal point of view. She couldn't proceed with her divorce or reconciliation.

She said, "I don't care where he is now, dead or alive, but I need closure. I am in limbo. He is simply missing, so I cannot remarry and I cannot dispose of his assets, even though there isn't too much. When we lost our jobs, or in my favorite metaphor, when our career boat hit a sand bar, he panicked. Eventually he sank our boat. But I didn't sink with him. I must survive because I have two kids to raise. I want to start a new life. So I am now waiting for seven years to pass to declare his death. Yashi, I am glad you managed well when your career boat hit a sand bar. Please pray for me to overcome my sand bar."

Last year, I read a newspaper article about a big wedding, Fran and a multi-millionaire. They would live in a beach-front mansion in Fort Lauderdale. The article mentioned that the newlywed couple planned to enjoy their sailboat. She will probably hit another sand bar in the future, but she will be able to keep her calm and survive on the rough sea of life again.

The Best Job Offer

" Yashi, I will double your salary, whatever you are making now," the voice said.
"Who is this? You must be kidding," I said.
"I am not kidding. This is Joe Green. Remember me? I worked for you about fifteen years ago. I need you as a vice president of my company."

"Oh, yes. You worked for me in our satellite telescope project, didn't you?"

After Davidson Manufacturing Company was purchased by Advantage Technology, all Davidson's facilities, where I had worked for the past fourteen years, would be closed and everyone laid off. The company was offering severance pay to employees who could stay until their official discharge date; they would not pay severance to employees who left before their discharge date. It was the late eighties and the era of downsizing and massive layoffs. I was fifty-nine years old, so I could stay with the company until laid off, collect my severance pay of thirty-five thousand to fifty thousand, and retire. I desperately needed a new job for at least another five years, because my youngest son was still in high school. When I heard Joe's offer, my reaction was, "Hallelujah, I am saved."

Joe continued, "Well, I invented a miniature satellite TV receiver and I now have my own company. You know I don't have too much academic background, so I need a credible vice president who could impress potential investors. My invention is a sure-fire big moneymaker. Are you interested?"

For the next two weeks we had intensive daily telephone conversations. Joe's invention could receive direct signals from a satellite and convert them for a television set. It was small enough to fit on the top of any television set without an outside dish antenna. He had already built a prototype with the seed money from a patron but needed more for second phase funding. The estimated potential market was one million dollars for the first year and 100 million dollars within five years. Furthermore I would get stock options, worth at least two million dollars after five years.

I resigned from Davidson and accepted Joe's offer. I didn't hesitate to replace my severance with the new opportunity of a million dollars. I left Boston on a Saturday morning for California. On Sunday Joe picked me up at the hotel and we went together to his company. In the demo room, a nineteen-inch television set sat on a table. There was another box, breadbox size, on top of the TV. It had a protruding, small black plastic sphere, like a tennis ball on top. Both boxes were connected by coax cables and power cords – nothing else. He turned on the power for both boxes and a clear picture showed in the television screen. I asked, "What's in the ball?"

"A super high gain satellite antenna, the heart of my invention, but I will not describe the details. My patent attorney advised me to keep it secret, since the patent is still pending. By the way, tomorrow at ten, some potential investors will be here, so I hope you will come over by nine."

"Yes, I will be here. Can I look inside the box?"

"Sure, go ahead."

I unscrewed the back panel from the box and peeked inside. It seemed to be an ordinary microwave receiver for satellite signals. I thought, "Wow! The plastic ball must be really a super high gain antenna, since it can make an ordinary receiver convert weak satellite signals to strong video signals for a TV set." I stood up on a chair to inspect the tennis ball more closely. When I looked at the top of the tennis ball, I felt an explosion inside of my head. I almost fell off the chair. I sat down with a terrible headache. I couldn't do anything more, so I immediately left for my hotel.

The next morning I arrived at his company early, despite a still lingering headache. "Joe, I am sorry I will have to miss the investors presentation this morning. I have to go home immediately. My wife became sick."

"Can't you stay another couple of hours?"

"Sorry, no. If I stay longer, I will not arrive home until tomorrow. Also I want to stay with my wife, so I have to resign from your company."

"You didn't like my offer? Ok, I will double your salary immediately, instead of waiting for three months."

"Sorry. It is not salary."

"Then what?"

"I hate to say it, but I smell a fraud."

"Are you crazy? Why do you say that?"

"At first I was impressed by your receiver. Then I got a headache. Remember? I never had that kind of headache before. So I thought very hard and now know the cause: your receiver. When I inspected the top of the tennis ball antenna, I suddenly felt a surging headache. High-energy microwave had to have hit my head. It means that your super high gain satellite antenna is getting strong signals from the ceiling, instead of weak signals directly from a satellite in the sky. Since microwave signals are invisible and there is no need of wires, it is a convenient way to deceive non-technical people. I don't know where there is a big dish antenna, but your invention is not what you claimed. Bye Joe, I have to leave now."

I was proud of myself, but thought I might regret later what I told Joe. I had no job, a terrible headache, a sick wife and many worries. I was headed back home without that million dollars.

Part Four
As a Family Man

With Invisible Escort

"That's the wrong bus! You have to take a No. 77 bus," I almost yelled at him; instead I kept my mouth shut and followed him into the bus. That was the first "solo" bus-ride for William, our eight-year old son.

The night before he had asked us for permission to go to Boston alone. We lived in Arlington, a suburb connected to Boston via public transportation system called the "T". I asked him where in Boston he wanted to go. He said to Logan Airport to see the planes. He loved to watch planes come and go for hours at a time since he was two years old. We had taken him many times to the observation deck of the airport, using the "T". He insisted he was familiar enough with it to ride alone. We knew our son had a strong sense of direction and geography. On one occasion, my wife Ann and I took him on a car trip to the White Mountains in New Hampshire. During the whole trip, he enjoyed watching outside scenery from his booster seat. On our return trip, we lost our way, where the road was not well marked. Our five-year old son, William, showed us the correct way home. We asked him how he knew that. He said that he remembered the particular trees and houses, which seemed no different to us from many others.

Ann and I had a lengthy discussion with him. In order to get to the airport, he would have to take a bus from our town to Harvard Square where he would pick up a Red line subway to the Park Street Station, then change to a Blue line and go to Scollay Square Station. There he would have to take an Orange line to the Airport Station, from which he would ride another bus to the observation deck. It was a daunting task even for adults. How could he manage? He was only eight years old. What would happen if he got off at a wrong station or took a wrong car? He said that he could ask and if he really got lost, then he would call home for help. The Boston subway system could be a dangerous place, especially Park Street and Scollay Square stations, where he had to change subway cars. They were located near Boston's notorious red light district. If a criminal abducted him, then what? Our son might have a special sense of geography and directions, but he might not have the social skills to handle such a situation. He insisted he could do it.

We argued a long time. He was determined to pursue his goal. Eventually Ann and he persuaded me to take a chance. Sooner or later we would have to let him go alone. Why not now rather than waiting for an unexpected event which would force us to a decision in the future. I was still uncomfortable, so we made a deal that he would be able to go alone, but I would accompany him as an invisible escort. He would go anywhere and do anything, but I would be behind him. I would not stop or interfere with his actions. As far as he was concerned, I would be an invisible stranger standing near him.

Three different bus lines passed through our town, but only the No. 77 bus went to Harvard Square. On the first step of his solo trip, our son took a wrong bus, No. 76, which connected to Lechmere Station, a streetcar terminal.

Because of our deal, I acted like a stranger, but I scrutinized his expression. He was enjoying the ride in a wrong bus and watching the changing townscapes. When the bus arrived at the terminal, he got off without a sign of surprise or panic. He inspected a wall map and stepped into a waiting streetcar.

I felt like I had completed a psychological hurdle race when he safely arrived at the airport observation deck. He had seemed to be having a glorious time watching planes taking off and landing and stayed there almost two hours.

On the return trip, he took the usual route. The last hurdle to reach home was a correct choice of No. 77 buses. The "T" adopted the same line number, 77, for two different destinations. Only the Diesel busses would go to Arlington. Even adults would often make a mistake in this choice. He stepped into an electric bus, the wrong one. The bus discharged us at the Cambridge Garage terminal. This was the fist time he showed a sign of surprise during the trip. He recovered quickly and asked the bus driver, instead of turning to me for help. So he got home safely about one half hour later.

When we arrived home, he was overjoyed and started telling his adventure to Ann. Meanwhile I was exhausted and had to take a rest before supper.

During supper I asked him, "Didn't you know that No. 76 bus didn't go to Harvard Square?"

"Yes, I knew," he said.

"Then why did you take the wrong bus?" Ann asked.

"I wanted to take a new route to the airport. The Harvard Square route was too familiar to me. Also I wanted to see how Dad would react when I didn't take the No. 77 bus."

My Wallet

"**D**ad, why are you still using an elastic band to hold your new wallet together? I thought your elastic band looked silly, so I gave you the new wallet for your birthday."

"If the elastic band offend you, I apologize. It was a nice present and I like it, but the elastic band is a necessary part of my wallet. I will explain it to you."

It started a long time ago, when none of you were born. Your mom and I went food shopping at the Broadway Market in Cambridge, the nearest supermarket. We found a parking space on the left side of one-way street across from the store. When I got out of the car, my wallet slipped out from my left pocket. It bounced once on the curbstone and fell through a narrow gap between the curb and the car. To my astonishment, it slipped into a small hole on the iron cover of a storm drain, which just happened to be immediately below the car. The wallet contained my entire week's pay, one hundred ten dollars, and Diner's Club and American Express cards; in addition to the usual family snapshots. These contents could be replaced, but it also contained my most important, irreplaceable possession, my green card, a legal immigrant registration card, the only tie between the United States and me. So I spent considerable time, effort and money, far more than one hundred ten dollars, to retrieve the wallet.

After the accident, I experimented with different styles and materials of wallets to prevent a similar occurrence. The best method I found was the use of a wide elastic band wrapped around the wallet, regardless of its material or style. It prevented accidental slips, because I had to exert a special effort to remove it from my left pants pocket where I always keep it.

From time to time, I heard comments from family members and friends about the elastic band on my wallet. I occasionally considered removing it for the sake of my family and friends. An incident in the Empire State Building, however, firmed up my determination to keep the elastic band as a permanent part of my attire.

A couple of decades back, I took several Japanese visitors sightseeing in New York City. One of our stops was the Empire State Building. At the entrance of the building were revolving doors. Some tourists seemed confused about the proper use of a revolving door. Sometimes more than one person ended up in the same compartment. There were several revolving doors and all were crowded. I guided my visitor friends one by one to separate compartments and pushed the door to rotate it smoothly. When I was ready to enter myself, a middle aged lady jumped ahead of me and entered the compartment. She annoyed me but it wasn't a big deal. I let her in the compartment and pushed the door. I entered the next compartment. Before the compartment was closed, a young lady, probably late teens, sneaked into my compartment. She made me uncomfortable. She was pointing the previous compartment and saying something in an unfamiliar language. They had to be together and the young lady upset about the older lady, I thought.

As if the older lady was responding to the younger, she turned around and tried to come back. The older lady was pushing back the revolving door in the wrong direction. The revolving door came to a standstill.

I shouted to the older lady, "Push the other way." I couldn't tell whether she could hear me or not, but she pushed harder than before. I pushed the door the correct way and she pushed in the wrong way. The young lady in my compartment also helped me to push the door the correct way. We played the pushing game for a few seconds.

I thought the old lady was another ignorant provincial tourist. I yelled to her and pushed harder. She said something and pushed back. The door didn't go anywhere. The old lady was strong. She was resisting the push of both of us. Suddenly I felt something. The young lady's right hand was in my pants pocket trying to remove my wallet with two fingers. Fortunately my wallet had the elastic band. She was trying again. I realized the setup. These people were pickpockets. What shall I do? They might have many companions. They might accuse me of harassing the young lady. My friends couldn't speak English. They could produce many witnesses, but I would be defenseless.

I slapped her wrist and yelled to her, "Don't do that!" Immediately the door moved in the correct direction. With my great relief, both ladies disappeared into the crowd without making any fuss.

Our Backyard

"What? You must be kidding!" George Irving screamed.

The town clerk repeated, "Sorry, Mr. Irving. Your development plan was rejected by the zoning board."

"Do you know why?" George asked.

"Yes, Windermere Street and surrounding areas will not be able to handle the traffic. There is no need to use the street to access your properties, since your plan included construction of a new road cutting through the middle of your property from Pleasant Street."

"That's sabotage! The road construction is the next phase of my development," George complained.

It was the middle of the nineteen-twenties; the Town of Arlington was rapidly changing from a playground for wealthy Bostonians to a bedroom town for blue collar workers for factories in Cambridge and Boston. Frank Windermere was an old school developer who built three story mansions with servant's quarters and separate carriage houses/garages. On the other hand, George Irving was a newcomer who specialized in low cost housing for blue collar workers. They had been feuding for a few years.

This particular feud started when George bought a sub-division of the Grey Estate adjacent to the Windermere complex. George snatched the property from under Frank's nose by paying an outrageous price. Frank had been planning to expand his existing complex with an additional five mansions. George's plan was to extend Windermere Street and to build twenty low cost two story houses with an integrated garage.

In early summer of 1970, we decided to buy a house and found an ideal house on Irving Street, Arlington. The street was a half mile long dead end street, starting at Pleasant Street climbing a hill westward. A roof-high rocky cliff blocked the end of Irving Street. Our house was the second last house among five similarly built two story houses, each having an integrated garage.

Since our house stood on a hill, we had three different levels of yards. A small front yard was at the same level as Irving Street. The middle level was a paved backyard which was the same level as the garage entrance and the basement floor. The lower level backyard was a large grass covered area, equivalent to the average size of two house lots. The front yard and middle level backyard were connected by a narrow driveway running at the side of the house, but the steepness and sharp curve of the driveway made it impossible to use our garage. A gentle slope continued from the middle level to lower level, with grass surrounded by trees and bushes.

Our house was located at the extension of Windermere Street, but the street was terminated by an eight foot high chain link fence which bordered our lower level backyard. There was no traffic between Windermere and our back yard, except for kids who sneaked around the fence and went through a gap between big silver maple trees.

Because of its location, our backyard was a safe haven for our own and neighborhood children. We installed a sturdy steel swing set and converted a rose garden to a giant sand pile.

The middle level was also useful for kids. It was a favorite basketball court and soccer practice ground. The garage door was an ideal goal or target for various balls:

baseball, soccer ball, handball, lacrosse, and ice hockey. However, the biggest attraction of our backyard was the sled coasting. Our backyard was on the north side of the house getting little sunshine during winter, so the deep snow stayed there for a long time undisturbed. Starting at the top of our driveway, they coasted from the middle level over to the lower level.

These old good days passed. All our kids grew up and started having their own cars. The number of cars in the family increased from two to three to four and reached five for a short while. We had to use the driveway and the middle level to park all these cars. This caused a big problem, especially on snow days. Once we parked on the middle level, we couldn't get up the steep and slippery driveway. After the snow stopped, we had to shovel the driveway completely from top to bottom and sand it. Then we could drive out one by one. In that time, we looked enviously at Windermere Street. We could easily get out in that direction, if there was no eight-foot high chain link fence.

More than ten years after all our three children left the house, we decided to sell. During an open house we spoke with a young couple.

"You look sort of familiar. Did I ever meet you?" I asked.

"Yes, I am Ralph Windermere, who used to live in the house next to your backyard. Your son, Kozo, and I played together in your backyard," the young man replied.

"Do your parents still live there? We lost contact with them", I said.

"No, they moved out, but they still own the house and now are planning to convert it to condos. We are interested in this house because it has a large tract of backyard which we might be able to make into parking space for the condos and also to build several more houses."

I was excited. It meant that the infamous chain link fence would come down and residents of this house and others may connect to Windermere Street. If their offer was reasonable then my wife and I were willing to sell our house to them.

Then his wife, Carla said, "You know my mother visited this house while she was a kid, because her great uncle lived here."

"What was his name?" I asked.

"His name was George Irving," she said.

It turned out that their bid was second highest, so we sold the house to them and contributed to the end of the Windermere-Irving feud.

Mike's Lucky Accident

Gloria heard a frantic voice on the phone, "Honey, it's me, at Community Hospital. Please come and pick me up right away. I had an auto accident on the way to work. I need a ride to my office. I have to attend an extremely important meeting." It was her husband, Mike.

"What happened? How badly are you hurt?"

"I'm not hurt at all, but my car was totaled. How soon can you come?"

"I can leave now, but you have to tell me what happened."

"Damn it, not now. I have to get to my office. This is my third day in the new job. It's a complicated long story. I will tell you while you drive me to the office."

Mike's new job was a forty-five minute drive each way. He had bought a commuting car from a newspaper classified ad, a used '69 Ford. It seemed to run well even though it had fifty thousand miles on it. The only concern was that it made slight clicking noises when he drove. He pulled into a gas station and asked a mechanic what the noises could be. He said it was probably the tires, frozen from being left outside overnight in the winter. Next morning when the car was driven, the tire would make noises because it was not a circle any more. Those noises would disappear after a little while. Mike believed the explanation.

On the morning of the accident, Mike had to leave home in the dark for an early meeting. He was doing sixty-five. There was no other traffic on the four-lane interstate highway. He turned on the radio, hearing an announcement, "Seat belts save lives!" He had heard similar messages many times, but had never used a seat belt before. It seemed sissy. That morning, he decided to try his seat belt. Once he put it on, he felt safe enough to test the new car for speed. He pressed the gas pedal. The speedometer needle rose to seventy, seventy-five…

Before it hit eighty, he heard a huge "Bang!" underneath the car and it began to spin out of control. He hung on to the steering wheel with all his might to avoid being shaken from the seat. His peripheral view showed one of the wheels rolling toward the grass divider in the middle of the road. The next thing he noticed was a car heading toward him on a head-on collision course. He couldn't control his car at all as it was sliding on the surface of the highway. Eventually he hit the guardrail on his right. The impact was considerable and he was shaken hard. He sat there motionless for a few minutes.

When his breathing returned to normal, he checked himself. Nothing seemed broken, and there was no blood. The seat belt had done its job. He tried the driver's door. It squeaked and opened. He stepped out and inspected the damage. The car had lost its left front wheel; the front end was touching the ground. The car hit the guardrail at an angle and the right fender was smashed but there was no damage to the guardrail. The car was sitting sideways: the front end near the guardrails and across the full width of the emergency lane, blocking about three feet of the right driving lane.

Full morning traffic had started and was still increasing. A Good Samaritan stopped, placed a flare behind Mike's car and called the state police with his mobile phone. Two state troopers' cars came and placed more flares. One trooper directed traffic to avoid Mike's car. The second trooper checked Mike's injury and the

condition of his car. While this trooper was calling a
towing company, the first trooper suddenly jumped on the
hood of his car. A passing Chevy sedan had sideswiped
him. The trooper seemed injured, crouching on his car.
The second trooper made a frantic call for help. The
Chevy that had hit the trooper pulled over and parked in
the emergency lane, a few yards ahead of Mike's car.
While looking at the Chevy they smelled gasoline; there
was a leaking gas tank, not dripping, but streaking. The
driver of the car, a tall skinny man about 20 years old,
said that he was on his way to a repair shop. The second
trooper called a fire engine. Mike asked the driver if he
had chewing gum and told him that chewed-up gum could
plug a hole in a gas leak. The driver pulled out a couple of
sticks, chewed them vigorously, and applied the blob to
the leaking gas hole. The leak was stopped. Several other
police cars, an ambulance, a fire engine and two tow
trucks arrived. The ambulance left with the injured
trooper.

The driver of the Chevy had no driver's license with
him and the car had no registration. The trooper put the
young man in a police car and left. The tow trucks pulled
away with the Chevy and Mike's car. The fire engine also
left the scene. Only the second trooper and Mike
remained.

The trooper told Mike that he usually wouldn't file an
accident report if there were no third party property
damage, or bodily injury. In this case a policeman was
injured, even though Mike had not directly caused the
injury, so he had to file a report. He offered Mike a ride to
Community Hospital since he had to go to there to see the
injured trooper. Mike ended up at the hospital, even
though he wasn't injured.

Mike's boss was skeptical about his story, but didn't
fire him. That same night snow started and accumulated a
couple of feet. Next morning, Mike walked to a

neighborhood dealer and bought a new car, a showroom display car, and took immediate delivery. He drove the new car to the towing company. Mike had to pay them a storage charge in addition to the tow charge. Furthermore, they demanded a disposal charge to scrap his car. In spite of those extra expenses, he didn't get anything from his insurance except a higher premium.

A couple of months later, Mike got a bill from the Department of Motor Vehicles for the repairing the guardrail. He filed a hearing request. At the hearing an investigator showed Polaroid photographs of damaged guardrails. Mike noticed that there was a snow bank in the photos, so he told them that the photos must have been taken a couple of days after the accident. The day of the accident was dry and clear with no snow on the ground. The snow had fallen during the night after the accident took place, so the guardrail damage had to have been done by a snowplow or by someone else, not by him. The investigator didn't buy Mike's argument, but he cancelled the repair bill, saying that a police report stated that there was no property damage.

Despite these troubles Mike was glad that he wasn't hurt at all because of the seat belt. This small accident became a turning point for the use of seat belts in Mike's family. Within less than a year, seat belts saved the lives of Gloria and their son Bob in separate accidents. Each totaled a brand new car successively within a two-month period, but both survived without any major bodily harm.

Licking Rock

Nathan crawled straight toward the open French doors leading to a big in-ground swimming pool. I was visiting my old friend John, having a conversation in his living room while John cradled his baby, Nathan. Soon the baby started to fuss and wiggle. He seemed to want his freedom. When John put him down on the floor, the baby creped away quickly. I wondered then why John was so calm despite the imminent danger. I was ready to chase the baby, if John wouldn't do it himself. When Nathan reached the door, he didn't keep going toward the pool. Instead he stopped and hugged a door stop, a rock as big as the baby's head. Then Nathan started to lick the rock. I had seen cattle licking a block of rock salt, but had never seen a baby licking a rock. After a few licks, the baby turned his face and smiled at John.

I asked John, "Don't you worry that the baby will fall into the pool?"

"No, he doesn't like the feeling of the tiles on the patio and never gets out of the carpeted part of the room."

"Do you know why the baby licks the rock?"

"No. As soon as he could crawl, he made a bee-line to the rock. He hugged, kissed and licked it. He loves the rock, I can say that," John replied.

It was not an ordinary rock. It seemed to be a fossilized plant and had pretty layers of yellow and brown. Later, I asked him, "Do you know what the rock contains?"

"No, but I believe it is harmless."

"John, I think it's better to analyze that rock. It might contain some toxic substance such as arsenic. I understand that arsenic has a sweet taste and is addictive. Did you taste it yourself?"

"Yes, I did, but it seems to have no taste."

"So it may not contain arsenic. Where did you get it?"

"It's a memento of my baby brother Ken. You remember Ken, don't you? I took it from his desk when I cleared his apartment after he didn't return from his cave exploration seven months ago. It was about the time that Nathan was born. I felt like Nathan was a reincarnation of Ken. When I saw he was licking the rock, I thought that this was a way Ken was calling Nathan to show his affection."

Then the phone rang and John took the call. He didn't say too much and listened carefully most of the time. Eventually he said, "Thank you," and hung up. He said to me, "That was the guy who was in charge of the search party for my brother. They completed the search and survey of the Devil's Hair cave complex but couldn't find my brother's body. That was my last hope of finding Ken. Now I have no idea what I should do. I need closure, but I spent so much money for the search. I am already up to my neck in debt. I'll have to devote the rest of my life to paying it back. I am sorry for my family, especially for Nathan. I won't be able to afford to send him to college."

According to John, Ken was an avid and expert spelunker who went on a solo exploration. Spelunking, that is cave exploration, is a dangerous sport, so a solo adventure is taboo just as in skin diving. Ken had called before leaving and told John of his intention to go alone. John believed that Ken had made a valuable discovery, potentially worth millions of dollars. So Ken didn't want anyone to know about it until he could secure it. Ken added that if John didn't hear anything from him within ten days, John should assume Ken had had an accident. John asked Ken where he was going, but Ken wouldn't tell him the destination, in spite of John's pleading. When John didn't hear anything from Ken, he had no idea where he should send a search party. John and Ken's fellow spelunker checked Ken's apartment for clues to his destination in vain. Since Ken and his colleagues had been exploring and surveying the Devil's Hair cave complex in New Mexico for the previous three months, John assumed he must be returning to that area. Ever since, volunteers and paid searchers had combed through the cave complex. John himself was not a cave explorer, but he joined the search every weekend and used all his vacation time. This last phone call indicated that the search party had completed the map of the Devils Hair cave complex and had looked in every nook and cranny, without finding Ken's body.

A few weeks after my visit, John called me with thanks for suggesting analysis of the rock. He said that the rock was a fossilized moss which grew on nitrogen rich substance, such as bird droppings. It contained high levels of phosphate high enough to be harmful to a baby. A doctor had given Nathan a series of de-phosphatization treatments. Fortunately Nathan was in only an early stage of phosphate poisoning, so that he was completely cured and didn't suffer any residual effect.

I said, "John, did your brother Ken ever go to any Pacific Island?"

"No, why?"

"The phosphate-rich fossilized mosses were valuable form of minerals that existed mostly in caves in Pacific Islands, where nitrogen rich guanos were abundant long ago. They are all exhausted now. So your brother might have discovered a new deposit in a cave. John, think hard! Did he ever go any islands or the seashore for exploration?"

After few seconds pause, John said, "Yes, he went on a business trip to Maine last year. He told me later that he explored an interesting cave while he was there."

"That's it!," I said, " A rare fish-eating bat lives on the Maine coast. Bats live in caves! Ken had to have discovered the cave. So try to find the cave where the bats live, and his remains should still be there."

A couple of months later, I received an announcement of Ken's memorial service from John. The enclosed letter told me that John had discovered the cave and also the body of his brother. Apparently Ken fell from a cliff and injured himself seriously. Without a companion, he could not get help and eventually died there. However, he wrote his will before he expired. Ken left all his estate to John, including mineral rights to the phosphate deposit. John assured me that the cost of Nathan's college education was now secured, courtesy of his uncle Ken. After all, Ken really was communicating with Nathan through his rock.

A Quality Life

The doctor came to her bedside and announced, "Katie, your X-ray shows suspicious growths in your colon and small intestines."

"What do you mean by suspicious growths?" she asked.

"They could be cancerous. When was the last operation? Five years ago, wasn't it?"

"Yes, my uterus and ovaries were removed five years and three weeks ago. I had a celebration party last week for five cancer-free years," she added.

"Only the biopsy can determine whether they are cancerous or not. I can schedule a biopsy next week, do you want that?"

"No, thank you. Instead, I would rather have the operation to remove them."

"Well, the problem is that they are too numerous to operate on. Even if they are cancerous, the only things we can do will be chemotherapy and radiation," he revealed.

"Then is it better to start these treatments right away?" she challenged him.

"Yes, we can, but they will make you sick. If you are willing to go through that, we can start right away. For your back pain, I have prescribed a stronger pain killer."

Katie had known that the recurrence would happen sooner or later. But the timing of the news disappointed her. She had come to the doctor for back pain, not for a semi-annual check.

She was aware that once the cancer spread to another part of her body, her life would end within six months. Therapy might prolong her life from two months to six, but they would not change the overall prospect. It was time to activate her prepared plan. She made a reservation for her bed in Hospice, and informed relatives and friends of her condition with business-like letters.

In some ways, Katie had been lucky. The initial operation was a success and she had lived five years cancer-free. During that time, she accomplished everything she wanted to do. She took care of her sick mother, who peacefully died in her arms last year. She helped her younger brother to remodel his house by using her share of her husband's life insurance proceeds. She learned to ride a motorcycle and enjoyed frequent cycling tours. All her children were married, independent, and successful.

Katie wanted to tell herself that she had nothing left to do in this world, except to live day to day as happily as possible, but couldn't convince herself. After she examined her mind carefully, she found the reason. It was a farm, her childhood dream. She had lived all her life in cities and never knew any farm life. During World War II her family had a victory garden, but she was too immature to be involved. Ever since, she had wanted to have a small farm and to grow her own vegetables. After she married she had been busy keeping house and raising children. They lived in condos in a city and had no land for gardening. Her desire to own a farm never had a chance to materialize.

While she was mulling over her farm she continued her therapy. Even with ten weeks of periodic hospital visits her health had deteriorated. Katie was getting weaker every day. She realized that if she wanted to fulfill her last wish, she had to decide quickly. She weighed the pros and cons of owning a farm and made up her mind.

She informed the doctors of her voluntary termination of therapy.

Katie rented a small cabin and a five-acre lot in the countryside. She moved in and started her country farm even though the cabin had no electricity or telephone. She got up every morning early and prayed. She was not a religious person, but she felt peace of mind when she prayed. She didn't pray for cure of her disease, but for one more day of life. Besides her normal farm work, Katie cooked her own meals on an old fashioned wood stove to avoid any prepared foods. At the beginning, she was so exhausted that she could hardly move by the end of day and went to bed. She was getting better and stronger day by day.

Occasionally, Katie had visits from neighbors, usually old folks, who were curious about an odd lady from the city living alone. They often gave her not only valuable advice on farming, but also helping hands for heavy work. An old lady, one of those visitors, suggested Katie try an herbal medicine, called "miracle bitter." It was made of leaves and roots of several different plants grown locally. Its bitterness was beyond description. She was not allowed to drink water, or any other liquid, for at least five minutes after taking it. For the first three days, the old lady supervised Katie taking the syrup. Katie continued taking the syrup partially out of curiosity and partially out of obligation to the old lady. By the third day, Katie sensed increasing energy and a sharpening of the mind. She continued the herbal medicine and eventually learned to make it by herself.

Her farm prospered and expanded to include two goats, a dozen hens, and a rooster. In spite of the hard work, Katie enjoyed life on the farm, living happily one day at a time. She forgot her sickness and other worries. She made peace with her body and mind.

About a year after she had started the farm, Katie went to the hospital to check her cancer; a day-long test procedure. While she was waiting for the result, her inner voice told her, "What am I doing here? Do I care about the result of the test? Will I change my life style, depending on the test result? No, I won't ..." She gathered her belongings, put on her coat, and walked out of the room. When she stepped out of the hospital, she heard someone calling her.

"Katie, wait. You have good news!"

The nurse ran after her, caught her breath, and said, "Look at this X-ray, there is no more cancer. You are cured."

"Is that so? Thank you," Katie said without emotion.

"Don't you want to see the doctor?" the nurse asked.

"No, thank you. I won't be coming back here again. Thank you for everything." Katie walked away.

Swimming

I felt elation from the morning sun shining on my naked body. Reflection from white sand was glaring in my unprotected eyes, even though the mid morning sun was not strong. I was lying on *Heta* Beach at the most exclusive resort in the country, located 100 miles from Tokyo, in the middle of *Izu* Peninsula, facing the Pacific Ocean. The beach was situated at the tip of a long cape. The outer side of the cape faced directly the Pacific and the inner side a bay that was connected to the Pacific through a narrow but deep inlet. The rough waves of the Pacific never arrived at the bay and the surface of the water was calm and as flat as a mirror. The coastline on this side of the bay was a sandy beach for the resort and the other side was a port for tuna fishing vessels. The mountains came close to the other side of the bay and a small fishing village clung to the bottom of the mountains. A narrow dirt road connected this resort to the village, but supplies came by sea on ferries. The only building in this resort was a large traditional Japanese style inn with modern accommodations such as individual rooms for all guests. Meals were excellent; locally procured seafood's were the freshest of fresh. Besides soothing sounds of waves, the only noises we could hear were occasional puffing sounds of fishing boats, going through the inlet. There were no cars and no trucks on this side of the mountains. There were no tourists. The climate was semitropical year round. It was a paradise. However, nobody could buy membership in this resort. The prestige and privilege were granted only to students of the University of Tokyo, the elite university of Japan.

It was the summer of 1955; I was enjoying this rare experience in my life. It had been a hard long struggle to enter the university, which was a guaranteed step to a successful career in Japanese society. I came from slums in Tokyo and I had never had this kind of luxurious experience before. I was enjoying this summer vacation in that exclusive resort. I was also taking swimming lessons, two weeks of intensive training with the best instructors. I had wanted to learn swimming before this, but somehow never did. While I was enjoying the warm sun I recollected a series of unfortunate circumstances associated with swimming, starting at my birth.

My father came from a rugged mountainside where the biggest water hole was a two foot wide, six inches deep creek. When he grew up he became a career soldier. The Army didn't care about swimming capability. My mother came from farmland where many small rivers and irrigation canals existed. However, her uncle had drowned in one of those rivers when he was a child. Ever since, my mother's family established a family tradition of a swimming ban. I grew up in areas where there was no pool or any other swimming place. When I went to school, none of my schools had a swimming pool.

Despite our non-swimming tradition, our family went to the seashore every summer, as a recreational one-day trip to *Ayase* beach. We took a two-hour train ride there. We rented a space in one of the many beach houses, changed to bathing suits and went to the ocean. At high tide, the water came almost to the edge of the beach house, but the water level never reached adult knee caps and the depth never changed for another mile or so. At low tide, you could walk miles on dry sand toward the water line. We also could dig clams, two different kinds: *hamaguri* and *asari*, on the beach. Our day at the beach meant that adults dug clams for supper and kids played with sand. I never learned to swim at the beach, despite many trips there.

A chance came when I was sent to my maternal grandparents' farm during summer vacations. Yes, that was the family with a swimming ban. Naturally they told me about the swimming ban and its background, but I frequently went to a river secretly with my friends of similar age. Eventually I taught myself to swim in the small river. Probably my grandparents were too busy with their farm work to monitor my whereabouts. Or they thought I would be safe as long as I went with my friends. My mother didn't know of my adventure. She trusted my grandparents. I couldn't tell my family that I could swim. Then came the first great opportunity.

It was during World War II, when I was in the fifth grade. The authorities decided to promote physical fitness for all pupils and swimming had to be one of the requirements. The whole class of fifth graders went to the nearest pool, an amusement park, a twenty-minute walk from our school. The park had already closed all facilities, except the swimming pool. I was excited about the swimming lesson, which would be my chance to authenticate my swimming capability without disclosing my secret activities during summer vacations.

It was an Olympic size pool, built for adult use only and most parts of the pool were too deep to stand up, especially for fifth graders. However, one side of the pool had a shallow raised underwater platform on which we could stand. All pupils from our class lined up at the side of the pool and then we carefully lowered ourselves into water while we clung to the edge of the pool with both hands. It was a relief that I found the platform, I could stand up on it, and my head was still above water. My position was near one end of the pool. The teacher stood at center poolside and gave us instructions: while we held the edge of the pool with both hands, to remove the tension from our bodies and let our bodies float. Then the bodies would float themselves, the teacher said. I tried it; it worked. My body floated. The teacher also told us how to kick both feet to provide the necessary buoyancy and locomotion. This was the most important part in the crawl, according to him. I had mastered the breaststroke in the river. I liked the style, because I could keep my head above the water. In the case of the crawl, I never managed to breathe while I was moving. But I knew how to kick my feet for the crawl. I could kick with stretched feet in rapid succession. So I was enjoying my floating body and kicking legs. I waited for the teacher to come toward me and give me praise for my kicking style. There were fifty pupils and he was giving advice individually starting from the other end of pool. I waited and waited for him while exercising my feet. As I kicked my feet more vigorously, I gained more confidence. At first I started to let one hand go from the edge of the pool, then I became bolder. I let both hands go for a moment. It was a violation of the teacher's instructions. He had insisted that we held to the edge with both hands. My experiment showed I could let both hands go and I could still float. The teacher was still far way. I became bolder and bolder. The duration of "no hands" became longer and longer. Finally I tried to determine how long I could float with no hands. I vigorously kicked legs and slowly let both hands go. Suddenly my body jerked backward. I panicked and tried to grab the pool edge. It was too far and I couldn't reach it any more. I panicked further. I didn't know what I did.

The next thing I knew was light green water surrounding me. I could see air bubbles rising upward. There was beautiful blue sky above my head. I was calm. It was eerily quiet, no sound. I was struggling for breath. I was choking for new air. I tightly closed my mouth and fought against the temptation to open my mouth. I imagined how comfortable it would be, if I opened my mouth wide and gulped air. I knew better. I resisted breathing as long as I could. I have no idea what I was doing. I was concerned about my breathing. I was maybe just standing on the bottom of the pool, or maybe struggling to go surface. I have no recollection. The only scene I remembered was bubbles and bubbles that were constantly going up. Finally I gave up and, overcome by the temptation of possible relief from the choking sensation, I opened my mouth, and gulped air, so I believed. It was water that rushed into my mouth. The choking sensation got worse and I lost consciousness.

Somebody pulled me up from the water. I was lying on the concrete floor and someone was asking me whether I was OK or not. I choked, coughed, and gurgled. Soon I was able to talk, "Yes, I am OK. Please don't tell anyone what happened. I don't want to be punished by my teacher and my parents." I stood up slowly and wandered toward a shed at the other corner of the ground. I hid myself there until the end of the session. I never knew who rescued me even today.

When I went home, my parents asked me how was my first swimming lesson. I said, "It was hard. I could hardly float myself." Fortunately they didn't pursue it further. The school decided to discontinue swimming lessons, due to inadequacy of the pool for beginners. From that experience, I acquired my life long fear of deep water, even though I never lost a strong desire to swim freely. I went to summer camps at the beach and took several short lessons at a pool during my high school years. I learned the physical skills of swimming, but I couldn't regain my self-confidence in it. When I entered college, I found another great opportunity to recover faith in myself.

In the post-war recovery era in Japan, we adopted every thing American. Higher education was no exception.

All public universities changed their names and copied the American higher education system. The former Imperial University of Tokyo, the topmost university in Japan, became The University of Tokyo and imitated many practices from Harvard University, the topmost university in the United States. An odd practice of Harvard was a swimming requirement for all graduates.

According to the story, a Harvard student, Mr. Harry Elkins Widener, drowned on the famous Titanic. His parents donated the then enormous sum of one million dollars to Harvard as a memorial to their son with two conditions attached. One was to build an academic library, called Widener Library, and maintain its original shape forever without modification, once it was completed. The second condition was that Harvard implements a graduation requirement for all students, the capability to swim at least 100 yards. Harvard gratefully accepted the gift, built Widener Library, and imposed a swimming test for all freshmen. Anyone who flunked the test was required to enroll in a remedial class and to pass the swimming test before graduation.

The University of Tokyo didn't build a new library, but it adopted the same swimming requirement with a minor modification; 100 yards became 110 yards, the distance of one round trip in an Olympic size pool. When I was admitted to the university, I took the swimming test along with other freshmen in a university pool. I was a borderline swimmer. I could swim the required the distance as long as I swam in the edge lane of a pool, but not in the center lane. My problem was not physical capability, but a psychological one. If I swam in the deep water, I needed something that I could grab in case of a panic attack. Without such a support, I couldn't swim in deep water. When I asked how deep the water in the pool was, people often teased me that the depth of the water didn't make any difference for swimming. I always wanted to correct my fear of the deep water. I regarded the test as a great opportunity to cure my phobia. I requested failure in my swim test, so that I could attend the corrective swim class. The class would be my second chance to become a real swimmer. At that time I assumed the class would be held in the university pool. A lucky break to me, it was held in the exclusive beach resort.

We had intensive swimming lessons for two weeks, two 2-hour session daily, morning and afternoon. Our class had fifty students, all freshmen from various departments of the university, a group of strangers from all over the country. Every one of us was there as a result of hard work, two to three years of concentrated preparation for and passing of the entrance examination, the toughest in the country. We were smart and intelligent, but lacked social skills. Despite being there two weeks, none, including myself, made close friends. Occasionally some played ping-pong or volleyball, but most of us spent our spare time reading books or studying, due to fatigue from the swimming lessons.

When the lessons were over, we had to take the final exam, a 1000-yard distance swim over deep water, from our beach to the diving pier at the east side of the bay. We were confident of making the long distance swim, because we had already tried a series of short distance swims, covering more then 1000 yards. The purpose of the final exam was to boost our confidence by swimming across the deep-water bay.

Two rescue boats manned by life guards were already at their positions about 300 yards and 700 yards away from the beach. We were eager to start. We lined up in single file, the shortest person at the front and tallest at the rear. We were walking into the water in tight formation, with almost no gaps between us. I was the 7th person from the front. I could hear some horseplay in the back of the line. Someone from the back yelled, "Move, Move."

When I reached chest deep water, some commotion started at the front, lots of splashes, but no voices. I assumed that the people at the front started to swim. I was ready to start swimming, but I needed space in front of me. I stopped and waited for the space. The person behind me pushed me lightly. I said, "Wait, I will move as soon as I have space." He pushed me again and almost knocked me down, but I firmly stayed in the position. He seemed to be being pushed from behind. I didn't want to push the person in front of me. The taller guys in the rear were eager to swim. I was again pushed forward from the back. I had to take a big stride, in order to prevent falling. With the big stride, my right foot couldn't find the bottom at the expected place.

Suddenly the water was above my head. Nobody expected the sudden drop of the sea floor. The instructor had told us that the beach deepened gradually, so we should start to swim when the water reached our necks. I had to swim at once, but I couldn't go forward, or back, because people were in front and back of me. I had no space to make a smooth transition from standing to swimming position. I had to get out of the crowd, otherwise, I would be drowned with them. I twisted my body and kicked bottom to thrust myself to the right of the file. Fortunately nobody bumped me or grabbed me. I successfully floated myself and started my breaststrokes. Then everybody seemed to be in a panic. I could hear lots of splashing sounds and meaningless gurgling noises, but I didn't hear any discernible words or screams. I swam as fast as I could parallel to the shore line, in order to separate from the crowd. Then I turned right toward shore. I glanced to my right in the direction of the crowd. I saw them bumping each other, several faces in and out of water. Their serious expressions were full of fear and desperation. They were, frantically moving their hands and doing lots of splashing. Judging from the angles of the faces, they were still in standing positions. They were so close each other that they had no way to start swimming. They were in a panic state. I hoped the lifeguards would come soon to their rescue. We were only a few feet from the shallows. I was not in any position to rescue them. I was barely swimming myself.

I continued my breaststrokes toward shore. I did not dare to stand up. If I stopped my strokes and found no sea floor I would never be able to float again. Finally bottom sands scraped my thighs. I crawled to the beach on hands and knees and lay there face down. It was the most tiring ten-yard swim of my life. I was so exhausted I felt like I just finished the planned 1000-yard long distance swim.

I didn't know how many minutes passed and what happened. When I raised my face slowly, I saw that most of the people were already on shore. Both rescue boats were also there. Some people were yapping like crazy and others were quietly standing like mindless ghosts. A little later, the instructor unsuccessfully tried to take roll call. A few people had already left the beach and returned to their rooms. He announced the postponement of the final exam to afternoon.

After lunch, our class met again on the beach and took roll call. We discovered one person missing. None of us recalled the person or was acquainted with him. We all had discussed the morning mishap during lunch hour. Nobody noticed his absence. A quick check revealed that he never ate his lunch, his room was undisturbed, his swimming trunks not found. The implication was clear. The exam was cancelled. Everyone was assigned to a search mission. We combed the beach to find any sign of him. Persons were sent to the village to hire boats. Officials were notified. Despite all efforts, we couldn't find any sign of him. Officials from the university and the village asked us many questions later. I felt bad because he was nonexistent in my memory.

Next morning we left the resort on a ferry. I felt strange because I had no grief for the drowned student. I was confused, but not sorrowful, probably because I didn't know him personally. My major regret was failure to regain my confidence in swimming. I wanted to swim without fear of deep water. My hope of confidence building was drowned with him. Well, I was lucky that only my hope, not I, was drowned. The ten-yard swim saved my life. It was a deep-water swim, even though it was short distance. I should be satisfied with the fact I survived, with or without the confidence. I later heard that local fishermen recovered his body with their bottom dragging net on the day after our departure.

A few weeks later I attended his funeral at his parent's house along with other students from the swim class. The general atmosphere of the place was close to that of my house: the bottom layer of residential areas in Tokyo. The busload of mourners was obviously out of place. I felt a strange kinship with the drowned classmate. He had struggled his whole life to get out of that slum with the full support and expectation of his family. He never had time or opportunity to learn to swim. I was sure that the swim class was his first chance to learn swimming. I was lucky that it was my second chance. Neither of us made it, but he was dead and I was alive. I had forever lost my chance to rebuild my confidence in swimming. I still vividly remembered the faces of drowning people, full of fear and panic, even though I didn't know whose faces they were. I didn't know whether one of them belonged to the dead friend or not. I was glad I was still alive and I had happily abandoned my desire to become a real swimmer.

Part Five
Any Job I Will Take It

Perfectly Legal

I saw him in the corridor walking with drooping shoulders and eyes on the floor.

"What's the matter, Harold?" I asked.

"I was laid off," he replied.

"I am sorry. We expected that, but not so soon. Do you have any leads?"

"No, but I am prepared. This job will be my last salaried work. I started a sideline business a few months ago. I will devote myself to it full time."

It was the early nineteen-seventies. Our project, a contract with NASA, was winding down and all members of the project had been anticipating the day it would end.

"What kind of business?"

"Distributorship for a detergent maker. Regardless of economic conditions, people always have to wash clothes. More than ten salesmen are now working for me. If I can double our sales force, I will make on commission alone much more than my present salary. In addition I am expecting to receive a bonus of $100,000 within six months. You will have the same benefit if you join my group."

$100,000 was big money, more than I could ever make in my lifetime. My weekly pay at that time was 110 dollars. "What are you talking about?" I asked.

"Well," he explained to me, "everyone who joins the group has to pay a franchise fee of $100 each to the Regional distributor." According to Harold, each salesman was obliged to recruit other new salesmen besides selling detergent. If he could recruit 10 salesmen, then he would automatically become a local distributor who would get a better discount rate for the detergent and collect commission for all salesmen within his jurisdiction. If you have 10 local distributors, then you would become a district distributor and 10 of them make you a regional distributor. Since every new salesman would try to recruit other new salesmen, the expansion of the sales network was automatic. Promotion on the ladder of distributor ranks would also be automatic.   According to Harold an average period to reach the next rank was about three months. He was already a local distributor, so he would become a regional distributor within 6 months and receive the $100,000 franchise fees from his new salesmen.

To me his sales group seemed to be a classical Pyramid scheme, in which each participant would theoretically get a large amount of money in the future. The pitfall of the Pyramid scheme was getting fewer and fewer new recruits. A quick calculation showed that when Harold became a regional distributor, the total number of salesmen would have to be one million.

I tried to explain to him, but he got angry.

"Yashi, think whatever you want. Even if I don't get the bonus, with commissions of a district distributor alone, I could make much more money than you make now."

Six months later I was laid off. The economy was bad and the Viet Nam War was getting worse. There was no hope for revival of space projects. I had several short-term jobs and was constantly looking for more security. Five years later, while I was walking down Mass Avenue after one of my unsuccessful job interviews, a car stopped beside me. Someone yelled to me through a rolled-down window, "Hey, Yashi. Is it you? I thought so."

It was Harold, and he was driving the latest model Mercedes.

"If you have time, hop in. I will buy you lunch."

He explained his success during our lunch at the Hotel Commander. His old marketing group went bust before he collected his bonus. He lost his house and his wife but he learned a lesson. He sued the executives of the group, collected some money, and used it to buy out the bankrupt group paying a penny on the dollar. He started a new sales company with several thousand salespersons. They still sold detergent and several other high-profit items such as women's cosmetics. He had a unique organization: a cooperative in which nobody received a salary. All associates — they don't call them employees — own the company stock. Everyone earns his income from sales commissions and dividends on his investments in the company. At that time the dividend was a minimum of 15% annually to a maximum of 30%, depending on the class of stock. There were 4 classes of stock, A, B, C and D. A stock had a selling price of 1 million dollars per share paying 30%; B stock, $100,000 with 25%; C $10,000 and 20%; and D $1,000 with 15%.

Each associate was allowed to purchase only one share of any class of his choice per month as long as he fulfilled his sales quota of the month. The strong motivation of the sales force came from this stock purchase privilege, Harold believed. This was the same kind of motivation as the pyramid group.

His story rang an alarm bell in my head. The scheme was complicated, but it was a Ponzi scheme: Paying old investors with new investor's money. As long as people bought new shares, the company could pay high dividends with the new money. Once new purchase stopped, the company would not survive for long.

He seemed to read my mind and said, "No, it is not a Ponzi scheme. This is a legitimate multi-layer marketing company with high profit and high dividends."

A few years later, I learned that his company, High Power Sales, filed for bankruptcy. The Mass. state attorney general investigated for possible illegal activities, because of requests from former employees of the company. However, the attorney general cleared them, saying that the company had never engaged in any illegal activities and officers were completely innocent.

I survived a few decades of hard work in low paid engineers' jobs without filing personal bankruptcy and finally retired to Florida with a modest pension. I think that was financial success on a modest scale.

One day a newspaper article caught my eye, reporting possible changes in personal bankruptcy laws. In one example, a convicted criminal, Harold O'Sullivan, had maintained a multimillion dollar mansion in Plato Island, Florida, despite several personal bankruptcies and fraud convictions. Florida law allowed him to keep his main domicile even in the case of personal bankruptcy.

Then I saw on late night TV an advertisement, "Seminar: How to make millions by investing in a multi-layer marketing company" by Harold O'Sullivan. It was him alright, even though he had aged. The speaker says on the screen, "Don't invest in stocks, invest in bonds, with guaranteed interest payment. Dividends can stop, but not interest payment from bonds. I will give you tips on how to choose companies. I made millions by investing in the right multi-layer marketing company. "

I didn't file personal bankruptcy and I am living in a modest manufactured home, but the person who filed for personal bankruptcy several time is living in a 10-million dollar mansion. Either my moral standard was wrong or

US economic principles were crooked. Maybe, I should take Harold seriously and should follow his advice.

High Return Investment

"One thousand times return, not one thousand percent return. No other investment will beat this kind of return," Joe said to me.

"Are you kidding?" I responded.

"No, I am not kidding. I personally made the thousand times return with my investment in stamps within two weeks. If you don't believe me, ask Greg. He will tell you it is true. Are you interested now?"

Joe explained to me that he syndicated an investment group for rare stamps. I would need to pitch in a minimum of one hundred dollars. He insisted that we could make at least five times that or five hundred per cent return within three months. I wanted to say "no thank you" immediately. One hundred dollars was big money for me. At that time, in the early nineteen sixties, I was making one hundred ten dollars per week before tax. Joe was my colleague but he was an old timer who was supposed to be teaching me the nitty-gritty of my new job. I didn't want to antagonize him. I said, "I have no money until I get my next pay check. Meanwhile I will think about it."

We were quality control representatives of our company who visited subcontractors periodically. We spent most of our time on the road. Fortunately I needed to accompany him only that once when he asked me to invest. I never told him my investment decision, because our schedule didn't allow us to meet face to face again.

Because of his investment scheme, I became curious about stamp collections. I read many books and even joined a couple of collector's organizations. Most stamp enthusiasts collected stamps as a hobby, but a few were involved in stamp investment schemes. Most stamp investments were based on rare stamps. Some rich collectors were crazy to acquire the rarest of rare stamps. As of the end of year the 2001, the highest priced stamp in the world was the 1854 British Guiana black-on-magenta penny stamp. The stamp was the only one of its kind. John Du Pont, the multi-millionaire convicted murderer, paid one million dollars for it. According to rumor, the investment syndicate which was its previous owner paid three hundred thousand dollars for it.

The most expensive United States stamp is the "Flying Jenny" twenty-four cent airmail stamp. The last asking price was one hundred thousand dollars. Behind the stamp is a classic moneymaking story. On May 14, 1918, a stockbroker's clerk in Baltimore, William T. Robey, bought a sheet of one hundred twenty-four cent airmail stamps at its face value, twenty-four dollars, at a local post office. He noticed the imprint of the airplane in these stamps was upside down, a rare printing error. He sold the stamps three months later for fifteen thousand dollars, six hundred twenty-five times the original purchase price. Every stamp investor dreamed of repeating a similar feat, but stamp investment is risky and large returns are rare. Like many collectibles, stamps have little or no intrinsic value. Market prices are listed in standard catalogs, such as Scott's, but actual prices are determined by auctions. Prices of rare stamps fluctuate widely, depending on the general state of the economy and mood of a few selected rich collectors.

Once I learned these facts, I stayed away from any stamp investments, but I became interested in stamp collection as a hobby. I collected stamps related to space exploration; more specifically United States unmanned satellites such as Echo and Telstar, because my work was in that field. In the late nineteen-fifties and early nineteen-sixties, most space-related stamps were issued by Russia and East European countries for Russian space triumphs, such as Sputnik, Rika, Vostok. Only a few countries issued a limited number of stamps of United States satellites. I estimated the total number of United States satellite stamps to be about several dozen, counting every country in the world. The best part of my topic was that only a small number of people would be interested, so the price of the stamps was reasonable, usually ten to twenty cents each. At that time, we didn't have any children and my wife worked as a nurse. I could afford to spend a few dollars and devote my spare time to stamp collecting.

That tranquil situation of space stamp collection changed drastically after the success of Apollo XI, Neil Armstrong's moon landing on July 20, 1969. Almost every country in the world issued its commemorative stamps, besides the United States. Many children and adults started collecting space stamps. That trend accelerated new issues of all kinds of space stamps in smaller countries whose revenue depended on sales of stamps. As a result, the total number of satellite stamps increased almost a hundred times and their price skyrocketed. At the same time we bought a new house, and had a new baby. Those changes killed my enthusiasm for stamp collecting, but aroused in me a new interest in stamp investment. I desperately needed more money.

I asked Greg for Joe's whereabouts.

Greg replied, "I hope you are not looking for an investment opportunity."

"Why?" I said.

"He was a crook. A couple of years ago, he gathered a total of one thousand dollars from seven people in the company. Then he said, 'Our investment went sour because the stamp we invested in was a forgery and had no market value.' The amazing part was that he offered a similar scheme to every new employee. A few of them became his victims. Eventually, he was forced out of the company because of his sideline business of phony stamp investment," Greg explained.

"Was his thousand times return story a lie?" I asked.

"No, it was true, but there was a catch. Do you know how much he made with the thousand time return?"

"No, I don't"

"Guess."

"Ten thousand dollars," I estimated modestly.

"Ha, everybody was hooked by the story. He sold his eight-cent stamp for eighty dollars. He made total of eighty dollars, a thousand times return."

Lost Christmas Present

"You might have won three million dollars," the stranger said on the phone.

I thought this might be another sales pitch. "I don't care. Whatever you are selling, I don't want it," I said.

"This isn't a sales call. I am Joe Fillippo of Gerald Microcomputer Co. You visited us at Christmas last year. Do you remember me?"

"Yes, but what is this three million dollar business?"

"Can you recall the day I picked your group up at the airport in my car? I stopped for gas. While we were waiting, I bought five lottery tickets for them as a Christmas present and gave one to each. I think one of the tickets is the winner of the three million dollar grand prize."

It triggered my memory. His car was a compact and we were squashed in it. I predicted to myself that the business deal we came for would fail because they couldn't afford a bigger car for foreign visitors. When he handed us those lottery tickets, we thought they were strange gifts even for a token Christmas present. The only thing we could do was to accept them individually. Each of us put one into the breast pocket of his suit; since we sat so close that we could hardly move our hands. As I predicted, the deal fell through and I had forgotten the incident.

"Why are you telling me now?" I asked him. "The lottery should have been drawn within a few days of our visit." According to him, he didn't pay attention to the winning number at the time of the drawing. Recently a newspaper had printed an article saying that the winning ticket for the three million dollars was unclaimed and it would become invalid after the next seven days.

When he saw the winning number, 5-7-10-12-18-19, a bell rang in his head. He recognized the number as one of the five lottery tickets he had bought for us. He had generated a five-number set based on the date and the year of the purchase: 5-7-12-18-19, representing December 18, 1975. All five tickets had the same five-number set, but the sixth number was different. It could be, 9, 10, 11, 13, or 14. It was derived from the time of purchase 9 A.M. We didn't know who had the winning ticket since we hadn't recorded which number was given to whom. The important thing was that we had to locate the winning ticket.

My customer file indicated that the four visitors were Messrs Abe, Baba, Cho and Dan from the Sun Instrument Company from Kyushu, Japan. At that time, I was on leave from my regular engineering job and working as an interpreter for visiting Japanese businessmen.

I also received a lottery ticket. I could be the winner. Where was my ticket? The obvious place was in the customer file, but it was not there. I usually never threw away any paper. I should have the ticket somewhere. I looked in all my drawers, business card files, miscellaneous boxes, pockets of suits and anywhere I could think of. I even looked through all books I read after that date, since I had a habit of using any kind of small piece of paper as a book mark. After a whole day of searching I couldn't locate my ticket. I realized it was lost forever.

In the same night, I made an international long distance call to Sun Instrument. I told a telephone operator that I was willing to talk to any one of the four gentlemen. Eventually I was connected to Mr. Dan, who was the lowest ranked among the four visitors. He was at first skeptical about my story, but I convinced him of its truthfulness. I emphasized that the time was short because the winning ticket had to arrive at the lottery office within four days. Even the fastest way, hand-carrying it in person, would take at least twenty-four hours.

Two days later Mr. Dan called me back and told me the whereabouts of all four tickets. Mr. Abe couldn't remember the incident, but his secretary knew the fate of his ticket. When he came back from the U.S., she emptied all the pockets of his suits in order to send them for dry cleaning. One of the items she didn't recognize, so she asked Mr. Abe about it. It was the lottery ticket. Since Mr. Abe didn't hear anything from me, he instructed her to discard the ticket. She threw it into a wastebasket.

In the case of Mr. Baba, he had vivid memories about his ticket. The day following the visit, he went to a bar at their next stop-over, Las Vegas, and gave his ticket to a bar companion. Mr. Dan believed the companion was really a call girl, since sleeping with a Caucasian girl was his secret but main purpose on that trip. Mr. Baba lost not only his lottery and airline tickets, but also his wallet that night.

Mr. Cho had died of a heart attack from the excessive stress of the U.S. trip, in which he had intended, but failed, to start a joint venture with an American company. Mr. Dan contacted Mr. Cho's widow and explained the situation to her. At first she insisted there was nothing in her home, since her husband never brought home any business papers. When Mr. Dan described to her the appearance of the lottery ticket and the possibility of its presence in the breast pocket of her husband's suit, she started to cry. Between sobs, she explained that because Mr. Cho's death was a result of the company trip, the company arranged his funeral. To symbolize his devotion to his company even after his death, she dressed him in his best suit, the exact same suit he wore during his American trip. Following Japanese custom, his body was cremated along with his suit, with the lottery ticket still in the breast pocket.

After a pause, Mr. Dan said, "I found my ticket in my scrapbook for the trip. I need your help, Mr. Nozawa. I would like to collect my money without informing the company. I will pay you for your trouble. How about ten percent?"

"Not so fast. What is the number on the ticket?" I said.

"It is five - seven - eleven - twelve – eighteen - nineteen."

"Oh, no! It isn't the winning ticket. The number eleven should be ten."

"Well, how much is the second prize for one number mismatched?"

"Yes, there is a second prize, but the amount is only one thousand dollars. It is not like the Japanese lottery, in which the second prize is up to eighty percent of the grand prize. In your case it is not worth the trouble of collecting it because a round trip air fare exceeds the prize money."

I was as disappointed with the whole incident as Mr. Dan was. A week later I received a letter from Mr. Fillippo with a newspaper clipping, informing me about the expired three million dollar lottery ticket.

A few years ago when I started to withdraw from my IRA, I needed to check my old tax records. Among my 1975 tax records, I found the lottery ticket bearing the winning numbers of 5-7-10-12-18-19.

Honesty Project

"Get Your $1000 Tomorrow: Researcher Plans One Million Dollar Give-Away," said a bold headline in the Metro Gazette. The article explained that Dr. Truman, a renowned psychologist from State University, was investigating human behavior. On January 15, tomorrow, his team would distribute one million dollars in cash to one thousand randomly selected people at one thousand dollars each. They would hand out a numbered plastic tag to any adult appearing in person between 9:00 a.m. and twelve noon at Treasure Hill Mall parking lot in the city. At one p.m. on the same day, a computer system would randomly select 1000 numbers of potential cash recipients. The tag holders selected would receive one thousand dollars on the spot, provided the person agrees to take a minor obligatory action.

The project had started at a posh restaurant in San Jose, at the peak of the dot-com boom, according to Dean, my boss. Aaron and Norm, who made billons from their own ventures, had a heated discussion on human honesty. Because they were drunk, their argument escalated into an unusual level of rivalry, despite Dean's effort to calm them down.

"A majority of Americans will become dishonest for a mere 100 dollars," Aaron said.

"No way, people are born honest. People in Metro City where I grew up handed in thousands of dollars of found money to the Police Department every year," Norm countered.

"I bet more people in the city kept their found money than the ones that reported it."

"Are you willing to bet?" Norm challenged Aaron.

"Sure, how much?"

"A million buck!"

Aaron upped the ante, "Are you chicken? How about ten million? Are you still in?"

"Of course, I am in. Here is my check for ten million," Norm placed his check on the table.

"Here is mine," Aaron did the same.

Dean said, "Calm down, both of you. This is crazy. There is no way to find out which of you is right and you are betting ten big ones on that."

"Hey, Dean. How about you become a judge and keep these checks," both Aaron and Norm said in unison.

Dean agreed. Later he drafted a formal contract with them and hired Dr. Truman to conduct the honesty test in Metro City. He also hired me as a project coordinator with the hidden role of auditor.

On January 15, Treasure Hill Mall parking lot was a mob scene. Some people came the night before and camped out to get the numbered tags. By noon, we distributed more than 20 thousand numbered tags. At one p.m., we posted the winning tag numbers for 1000 potential recipients.

Holders of tags were led into a big room where a researcher interviewed each tag holder to explain the procedure to get money. Each winner would get a credit card in exchange for the tag. Then he or she would go to a special ATM machine in the adjacent room, key-in his or her name, address, and telephone number and receive 1000 dollars cash and a printed form. The person then would go to the next room to read the form. The interviewer could not disclose the contents of the form, so recipients would have to read carefully. If they would agree with the contents, they would have to sign the sheet.

If they wouldn't agree, then they would have to return the cash into a deposit box.

When recipients entered the reading room, they would understand that they could leave the building through exits without being seen or challenged by anyone, if they wanted to ignore the procedure after they received the cash.

The form explained what we called "the minor obligatory action." Recipients of the cash were asked to donate a minimum of five hundred dollars to their favored charity within thirty days. If they agreed, they had to sign the sheet before leaving the building. They were to take the signed sheet with them, because they had to send the form to the charity along with the money.

The implication was intended to be clear to all recipients. Each had three choices of how many dollars they could keep: nothing, five hundred dollars or one thousand dollars, depending on the decision to be honest or dishonest.

To study their behaviors, we had installed hidden monitoring devices and sophisticated computer systems to study their identities, facial expression, and body language. As a result, we successfully uncovered identities, behaviors and financial condition of more than 95% of recipients by the end of the project.

Three years and five million dollars later, Dr. Truman published the results of the honesty project in a reputable academic journal. His article claimed that more than 95 % of people were dishonest with the temptation of one thousand dollars. This report stirred academic, religious, political, and ethical circles. I submitted an audit report to Dean, prepared by an accounting firm which I had hired. They showed that Dr. Truman's conclusion was not correct. He had manipulated the data to show that 95% of people were dishonest, but the actual results could be as low as 45%. Furthermore, the project financial report filed by Dr. Truman included more than one million dollars of irregularities. So I wrote Dean that results of the Honesty Project were inconclusive because a dishonest person, Dr. Truman, said that people were dishonest. Soon after that I got a new job and moved on.

Dean retired to Florida and was living near me. During a visit, I asked him who won the bet, Aaron or Norm.

Dean said, "Neither. The bet had been off for a long time before completion of the project. After the dot-com boom burst, both Aaron and Norm wanted to cancel my contract and recover their money. I settled with them by returning five million each, so they were happy and didn't care about the results of the study. I got a fat fee and you, Yashi, got a job with good pay. Truman got lots of research money. Nobody cared about the result, but everybody is happy. The purpose of the honesty project was just an honest business deal, as far as I am concerned. Don't you agree?"

Andy, the New Sheriff

"Stop," Andy screamed to the driver who was backing up their truck from a narrow blind driveway into the street. Andy thought that he detected something moving behind the truck. He opened his door, jumped out of the truck, and ran to the back. A small girl, probably five years old was running after her ball toward the truck. Andy was just in time to grab her and prevent her from going under the truck. The girl was frightened and started to cry because a stranger had suddenly lifted her from the ground. Andy was also confused and he didn't know what he should do next. Then he noticed that a middle-aged lady was running after the girl while screaming something unintelligible.

Andy wondered why the girl didn't stop when she heard the beeping sound of warning from the backing truck. The lady who was out of breath thanked Andy and told him that the girl was deaf and she was the babysitter. Because of the commotion, several people stopped and gathered around them. Since it was at the back entrance of a bank, and an armored car was sitting there with its door open, somebody might have called 911. Soon patrol cars arrived with a news-reporter not too far behind. The next day's local newspaper included an article, "Alert Guard Saves Deaf Girl's Life," and Andy became a local hero. The big story was that the deaf girl was a granddaughter of the newspaper publisher.

The incident had happened during a short period while I was working for a security company as a temporary guard. Andy was my colleague, or maybe a rival, and our job was to deliver bags full of cash to different banks. Andy and I worked for different teams, even though we had the same function. Andy was soon hired as a permanent employee after the publicity. When I heard this news, I was upset at the unfairness of the world. Andy was not a hero, but a negligent, lazy bum in my opinion.

I asked Andy, "Didn't you know that you violated the operational procedure by keeping the truck door open while helping the girl?"

"Sure I knew it, but think about it. Which is more important: saving the girl or sticking to the procedure and run over the girl?" he replied.

"You were right. Saving the girl was more important than sticking to the rule. But if you had stuck to the procedure by staying outside the truck during the backing out, the incident would never have happened, don't you think?"

"Aha! That's the difference between you and me. You want to stick to the pre-determined procedure under any circumstance, but I am always looking for a chance to break the rule. I will explain why. The reason our company issued the procedure was that they didn't want a security breach. You agree, don't you? Now think carefully. If a security breach would never occur, what will happen? All customers would think there is no need to hire an armored delivery service company like us. So we need an occasional security breach to remind our customers of the need of our service. The deaf girl incident was not exactly security breach, but the publicity helped our company and my reputation. For your information, the incident was not completely unexpected. I knew that there was a posted sign saying, "Deaf Child." I just grabbed the opportunity to promote myself. This world is built for smart guys like me, not for the earnest guys like you."

I realized that that company was not the place for me to work, and soon after I was fired from my job. A few months later, Andy appeared in the newspaper again. This time he was a hero who foiled a bank rubbery. He had shot and killed a suspect. According to the story in the paper, the suspect, who was a drug addict, had hidden near the back entrance of the bank, and waited for the arrival of Andy's cash delivery truck. When Andy was carrying a cash bag, the suspect jumped out, hit Andy with a club and grabbed the cash bug and fled. Andy, who had been delirious from the concussion, pulled his gun and fired several shots toward the suspect. One of the bullets hit the heart of the suspect and killed him instantly. The article carried photographs of Andy and also the suspect. When I looked at the suspect's photograph, I felt some kind of familiarity with his face, but I couldn't pin down who he was.

About one year later, Andy ran for the office of Town Sheriff. He was successfully elected by an overwhelming majority. The newspaper again listed his many accomplishments and one of them was the foiled bank robbery. When I read the article again and examined the accompanying photograph of the killed suspect, my mind suddenly clicked. I remember who he was.

Several days before the bank robbery, while I was looking for a new job, I had completely lost my way to a new prospective employer. I was in the desolate part of the town and I was desperate to find a place to ask directions. I saw a sign for a bar, a very shady looking establishment. I felt uneasy about going in, so I was sitting in my parked car and thinking it over. Then I saw Andy coming out the bar. I thought that I was lucky to meet him there and I could ask him for directions. He had a companion who was not like his typical friends. His companion was shabbily dressed and looked like a homeless person. Because of his companion, I hesitated to call Andy. Meanwhile, Andy rushed to his car and drove off. His companion walked away from the bar and passed my car. I had enough time to look him over carefully. The most unique part of the guy was a big scar on his face; his forehead to left cheek across his left eye.

The photograph of the suspect in the article clearly showed a scar from forehead to cheek across his left eye. I didn't know what I should make out of the coincidence, but I was glad that shortly after the election I moved out from the town to another sate, which was far away from the jurisdiction of the new sheriff.

Missed Thanksgiving

Every year at this time, I mourn for Pilgrims and thank God for my accident. It started when I decided to become an Indian in the early nineteen-nineties.

I took a new job as vice president of engineering in a small privately owned company, Killdoer Tech, in New Hampshire. Employee's attitudes toward work and recreation were different there, compared to those in my former job in Massachusetts. Most of them lived in rural areas and enjoyed outdoor lives. The most popular sport was hunting and many people had shooting ranges in their own backyards. On the opening day of hunting season the company was almost deserted. Many long-time employees took the day off. When I complained, they said that it was a company tradition started by Mr. Killdoer, the owner.

He had successfully managed the company for thirty years, but its business was turning sour lately. He hired a new young president, Hunk Savage, who assembled a new management team, including me. According to rumor, Mr. Killdoer gave Hunk carte blanche to rebuild the company. Hunk fired a group of old-time employees, many of whom were personal friends of Mr. Killdoer. When I was hired immediately after the layoff, the company was in turmoil. The remaining employees naturally identified me as one of the cruel new breed, exemplified by Hunk.

Strangely, my first encounter with all employees would be handing out frozen turkeys on the day before Thanksgiving. The tradition began the year the company was founded and had continued ever since, despite the fact that a few employees didn't want turkeys anymore; some wanted hams and some cash. Hunk wanted to abolish the custom, but the owner insisted that each turkey cost two dollars at wholesale and the goodwill among employees was worth many times that. Hunk argued that it was not money, but time and effort that management had to spend. Furthermore, the expected goodwill among employees was doubtful, especially following the previous year's mass food poisoning from frozen turkey, even though none were from our company. Eventually Hunk and Mr. Killdoer agreed that this would be the last year, because the turkeys had already arrived and couldn't be returned.

One tradition in the turkey giveaway was that all members of management, seven of us, were to dress in Pilgrim costumes as we handed out a turkey to each employee. I thought this would be an opportunity to establish my image among employees as an innovative, non-conforming, kind and friendly manager. I decided to become an Indian, instead of a Pilgrim. I called up all costume rental companies in the local yellow pages for an Indian costume. None was available. They said, too late. I should have made a reservation earlier. A week passed in vain. It was Tuesday afternoon. I was desperate. I called again the same costume rental companies to ask about cancellations. Eventually I found one in Manchester.

The next day, Wednesday, we had to hand out turkeys, I had to get there promptly. It was almost 5:00 pm and the shop closed at 6:00 pm. I jumped in my car. The traffic was building up on the local two-lane street I had to take before getting on the highway. I was irritated. Finally I could see the corner at which I could turn off to the highway. My lane was jam-packed, but the opposite lane was empty. No cars were coming in the opposite lane. It might be illegal and dangerous, but I thought I could make it. I steered my car to the opposite lane and gunned it to reach the corner first. Suddenly a red pickup truck appeared from a hidden driveway. It would be head-on. I cut my steering wheel to the left to get off the road, but too late. The truck hit the right side of my car. I felt the impact and I lost consciousness.

When I woke up, I was in a hospital bed. I had a throbbing headache and dull pain all over my body. The first thing that came into my mind was the turkey handout. I cursed my bad luck and blamed the red truck. It was my first big appearance before employees. I had lost my opportunity. The next time I woke up I saw my wife at the bedside. She said that I was lucky. If the truck had hit my car a fraction of a second sooner it would have crushed me. My injuries were a concussion to my head and a compound fracture in my right leg. But I survived. Thankfully the doctor said that I would recover within three months with no permanent damage.

I had missed my family's get-together at Thanksgiving, when all three kids came home for the first time after their departure to college. In addition to that I had lost the opportunity to show off in the company turkey handout. I wondered what I did, or didn't do, to deserve this kind of treatment from God. It was supposed to be a memorable Thanksgiving, but turned out to be a miserable one. I spent it in a hospital bed, unconscious.

Then my wife asked me, "Is your company called Killdoer Tech?"

I said, "Yes."

"I thought so, but I wasn't sure."

"What's the matter?"

"It was in the TV news all over. There was a murder-suicide there," she said.

We turned on a hospital TV. The newscaster said that a disgruntled former employee visited the company during the annual turkey handout with a shotgun and a rifle and attacked the company management team. Mr. Hunk Savage, the president and two managers were dead and three were critically injured. The former employee killed himself. The TV screen showed scattered blood-stained Pilgrim costumes and lots of frozen turkeys.

If I were there I would definitely have been killed because I was part of new management. Due to my accident, I wasn't there and it saved my life. Despite lots of pain and aches, the fact that I could see and touch my family was my real feast on that Thanksgiving. Thank God, He acted mysteriously.

Red Convertible and Silver Jaguar

T he new red convertible in our parking lot surprised me. It was the only shiny car among more than a hundred dust-covered vehicles, most of which were semi-wrecked station wagons or battered pickups, mixed with a small number of low-cost imports. Most of them showed the battle scars of severe winters and unpaved roads in rural New Hampshire where our company was located.

The real surprise was that it was parked in the spot designated for Mr. Ketchum, our autocratic company president, who had been driving a ten-plus-year old Ford station wagon. His employees thought he was a tight-fisted control freak. We had to get his signature for all purchase orders, even for a five-dollar stapler. He didn't tolerate any infringement of rules and procedures. He would fire anyone who parked in his space, even though none of the parking spaces were marked. He had assigned all parking spaces according to the pecking order in the company. Everyone in the company knew Mr. Ketchum's space. Only strangers, often innocent customers, parked in his spot, because it was the most convenient space.

Doubt about the owner of the red car quickly disappeared. A guy from the Production Department insisted that he had seen Mr. Ketchum driving the car that morning.

Speculation as to why he bought this new car, instead of another utility type automobile, flourished among the employees. They agreed that he was ready to buy a car, probably because his old car broke down, but there was no acceptable theory as to why he selected a convertible. Yes, he could afford it, but it was out of sync with his known character.

A young lady from Accounting revealed a hidden-side of Mr. Ketchum's character. She said that he often rented a flashy car when he was on the road. He might prefer driving a sport car, even though he had owned a station wagon or something similar as long as any employees remembered. An old-timer confirmed the hidden side of Mr. Ketchum's character. He said about ten years ago, when Mr. Ketchum's pickup died, he drove a Thunderbird to work for a few days before he bought a Ford station wagon. That explained it, we thought. We expected to see another station wagon or pickup the following week.

To our surprise, Mr. Ketchum drove a brand new silver Jaguar the following Wednesday and every day thereafter. This new development stimulated the rumor mill in the company. Some said he won the lottery. Many believed he received a substantial amount of inheritance from his widowed mother who had died a few months earlier. Many employees were interested not in the source of his money, but the reason for his change of character. The second wave of rumors spread within the company.

One story had it that Mr. Ketchum had a young mistress or a girlfriend, because someone saw him driving with a woman in his Jaguar. Dave from the QC Department augmented the speculation: his wife's girlfriend knew a young former model who told his wife that the model was dating a sixty-two year old president of an instrument manufacturing company in New Hampshire. His wife believed that the old man had to be Mr. Ketchum.

Frank from the Purchasing Department insisted that sickness was the cause of Mr. Ketchum's change. Frank's daughter, a nurse, believed that Mr. Ketchum was a patient at her hospital, who had lung cancer. The doctors recommended immediate surgery and chemotherapy, but to their dismay, the patient discharged himself to avoid treatment. According to her, the patient would live at most twelve months. She believed it was Mr. Ketchum, based on a photograph, even though she neither remembered the name of the patient nor ever knew him before. We knew Mr. Ketchum was a long time heavy smoker.

Shortly after the incident, I left the company for a better paying job. At that time, Mr. Ketchum was alive and driving the Jaguar every day. Several months later at a banquet of a technical conference, I shared a dinner table with Ms. Pamela Ketchum, who was a computer expert. I asked her whether she was related to Mr. Ketchum, the president of a New Hampshire company. She said yes, she was his daughter. So I asked her about the puzzling Jaguar.

Pam explained that her father loved driving a sporty car, but he always bought a utility-type automobile to please his mother. He was the only child of a widowed mother, who raised him throughout the Great Depression. He respected her opinion and consulted her about almost everything, even after he married. He always tried to please his mother, who was a lovely, kind person, but frugal and intolerant of unnecessary expense or frivolous items. In the case of an automobile purchase, Mr. Ketchum's mother always expressed her strong preference for a pickup truck for its versatility and ruggedness. Pam's father had always valued advice from his mother whenever he needed a new car, because it was such an expensive purchase. When he became the president, Mr. Ketchum wanted to buy a new automobile to suit his elevated social status. Grandmother objected, so her father followed her advice and kept an old pickup.

When Pam became a teenager and a licensed driver, she wanted to drive a car, especially a Thunderbird. At first, she unsuccessfully tried to persuade her father to buy one for her. Eventually her mother and she persuaded her grandmother to approve of her father buying a station wagon, which could do a job similar to a pickup truck in a much more elegant way. According to Pam, it took almost twenty years to get grandmother's approval to buy the wagon.

When Mr. Ketchum's mother died, Pam and her mother encouraged him to buy a new car. They wanted him to select a Lincoln, a Mercedes, or something suitable for a company president, not a Ford station wagon. When he chose a puny Miata, the poor man's sports car, for a test drive, her mother hit the ceiling. She said his choice showed immaturity caused by long suppressed childish desires. It was inappropriate for his social status. Pam also concurred with her mother. She and her mother suggested that her father buy a Jaguar, which matched his social status and was still sporty. He obliged them and everybody was happy, according to Pamela Ketchum.

A Prisoner of Love

At lunch break, it was snowing with several inches already on ground. Gene, my colleague, was putting on his snow boots. "Are you going home?" I asked.

"No, I am going for my daily exercise walk."

"With this snow, you are crazy."

I knew he might be an oddball, but not crazy. He was near my age, early fifties, but he would pigheadedly pursue something once he decided on it. When he made up his mind to take a daily exercise walk, he was different from others; he never skipped a day, regardless of weather, schedule conflict, or any other obstacles.

When he was ten years old he wanted an expensive model airplane costing twenty-five dollars, a real flying machine with a gasoline engine. His parents couldn't afford to buy it. His father said, "Even if I could afford it, I wouldn't buy it for you. It is a waste of money. You'll be tired of the plane within a few weeks and want another new toy."

He replied, "Dad, I really want the plane and I won't need any more toys from you. I know it is too expensive to ask you to buy for me, but is it OK with you if I find a job and earn money for the plane?"

His dad was astounded by his determination and said, "Alright you may find a job, but you must maintain good grades in school. You won't get any more toys, even at Christmas, until you get your plane."

He found odd jobs in the neighborhood and delivered newspapers, never complaining or asking for another toy. Even his parents were surprised at his stubbornness. After two years' struggle, he saved up enough money and bought his plane. The arrival of his long-awaited treasure didn't end his tribulation. After he finished assembling his model plane, he found that its engine didn't start. When he rotated the propeller with a finger, he expected the engine to catch and fire itself. But it didn't. He read the instructions again and repeated the procedure, but it didn't respond. He thought he might not be rotating it fast enough, so he pulled one side of propeller harder. The engine seemed to start momentarily, but didn't continue. He was encouraged. Trying to pull harder, he cut his index finger with the edge of the propeller. He changed fingers, but it was too awkward and he couldn't pull as hard. He got a winter glove and wore it on the right hand to protect the crease of the index finger. He wouldn't stop until the engine started. His arm was getting tired and his hand was so sore that he thought his index finger would fall off any moment, but he didn't stop. Whatever happened, the engine suddenly puffed a couple of times, spit out black smoke and roared by itself. He jumped and yelled with joy. He had spent more than five hours trying to start the engine.

When he was in high school he fell in love with Josephine. She was raised in a well-to-do, strict old-fashioned family and he came from a poor family. Gene thought her father would never approve of him. They met only in school during breaks. Both swore to spend their future together. When they were ready to graduate, they decided to obtain formal approval of their relationship from her father.

Her father didn't allow any kind of courtship between them and insisted they come back after graduation from college. Gene and Josephine agreed to wait for marriage until graduation, but they begged permission to maintain their friendship. They argued with her father that an unattached college student would find opposite sex friends who would be strangers to the parents. It was unrealistic and a source of future disappointment if parents expected their daughters to stay clear of any boyfriends throughout four years. On the other hand, if Gene was always available for Josephine, she wouldn't be likely to find a new boyfriend when social activities required male partners. Maybe her father saw Josephine's love for Gene. When he reluctantly gave permission for courtship, he sternly warned them that her virginity would have to be maintained until marriage, not only for her honor but the family's honor as well. In gratitude to Josephine's father, Gene promised that he would preserve their honor forever. Shortly before their departure for college, sickness struck Josephine. It started out as simple fever and headache, then persistent coughing. At first Gene visited her every day, but he was isolated from her by doctor's order when her paralysis appeared. He wrote a letter every day. In those letters, he promised her many times that he would wait her for complete cure, even if it took forever. Some could say that puppy love blinded him and temporary insanity took over his brain. As far as Gene was concerned, he really meant it and he took his promise seriously.

Unfortunately for them, the doctors found that her disease was incurable and the paralysis was permanent. Furthermore she would have to live in the isolation ward until the day she died and would never return to the normal world.

According to Gene, those events took place about thirty years before we met. In our office, people gossiped about the true reason for his determination not to marry. His friends, including myself, didn't dare to say but secretly thought that he might be gay. I didn't pursue this subject, so I don't know the real answer. He seemed straight based on my superficial observation. There was even a rumor that he had a mistress and had children with her. Another rumor was that his determination had nothing to do with his engagement to Josephine any more. It was based on external pressure from Josephine's father. Gene had sworn a blood oath that he wouldn't marry anyone else except Josephine. The oath couldn't be broken under any circumstance, or he might be killed because he sullied her father's honor.

I knew that he still longed for Josephine. The road we used for lunch time walking was popular with employees from other companies as well as ours. They often walked in groups of five or six abreast, because the road was wide, paved and no traffic. So we saw many other people walking in the opposite direction, including many lovely young ladies. When he saw a girl resembling Josephine he talked about her -- how lovely she was and how sweet her voice was.

Once I left the company, we didn't communicate again. A few years ago, I got a letter from his sister. It said that Gene died from cancer and my name was on a list of people he wanted notified. I called her and expressed my condolences. I was also curious about his circumstances. His sister, who was more than twenty years younger than Gene, was the only surviving kin and his substantial financial assets were left to her and only to her. When I asked her about Josephine, she said that she had never heard the name.

Part Six
After Retirement

How Not to Make Money

A shabbily dressed woman asked me, "Are you throwing away this figurine?" I never saw her before, but she might have been one of junk collectors who flock around in the morning of rubbish day. She was pointing to a clay horse standing at the top of our junk heap in front of our house. We had sold our house and we had to empty it out by the next day. It was our last chance to dispose of unwanted items without paying for removal. All necessary or keepsake items had been shipped to our new house in Florida, which has one-tenth of the floor space of the old house. We had to dispose of most of our forty year's accumulation. The next day the dump truck men would take everything away at a dollar per pound. I had no time or space to keep anything else except items already loaded in our cars.

"Yes, you can take it if you like. I don't have time to look for a buyer. If you find the right buyer, it may be worth fifty to a hundred dollars."

"I don't know anything about the figurine, but I thought it was odd looking. Can you tell me anything about it?"

"It is called a *Haniwa* horse and it's more than fifteen hundred years old. *Haniwa* is a general term for clay figures made around the fourth to Fifth century in Japan for decoration of tombs of noble people. This twelve-inch horse is unusually large; they are commonly five to six inches. If you look carefully, you will notice it has a cow's hoof instead of horse's on the left front foot. Because of these two unique features, it might fetch a much higher price, if and it's a big if, you find the right buyer/collector. I got this horse from a Japanese scholar who stayed at our house while he was visiting Harvard. Since he was an archeologist, I believe this is authentic, although many imitation *haniwa* exist. So take it with you and try to make money from it. Good luck."

I had completely forgotten this incident which happened a few years ago. I am now happily living in the Sunshine state. One night recently I got a call from my son, Robby.

"Look Dad, go to e-Bay, you know the auction site. People are bidding on a clay horse just like we had at our old house. You won't believe the price. It already passed fifty thousand dollars. Do you still have the horse?"

"Well, Robert. Sorry to say I don't have it anymore. Also it might not be the same horse. What does the description say?"

"It said that it was an ancient Japanese clay horse, called *haniwa*. It was a large specimen, twelve inches high, compared to the usual five inches. Excellent condition. It has the unique feature of cow's hoof in front left foot. According to a Japanese scholar, it was made in around 375 AD and its cow's hoof indicates its origin was in an imperial tomb. The only other known specimen exists in the Japanese Imperial collection."

"It might be the same horse we had."

"What did you do with it?"

"I gave it away to a strange woman. Or more correctly I threw it away as rubbish and she picked it up."

"What? You threw it away? Why didn't you give it to me?"

"Well, too late now. I gave an opportunity to you and all other my children. I told you that you all could take anything you want from our house. But nobody wanted the horse."

"Then you should have sold it yourself. Didn't you know the value of the horse?"

"Yes, and no. I knew it was worth something, may be ten to twenty dollars for anyone interested. If I spent lots of my time to find the right dealer or collector, it might fetch one hundred to five hundred dollars. I didn't have time or energy for such a project. I wanted to enjoy my limited time in Florida as soon as possible. My only concern is whether the poor lady got all fifty thousand dollar plus or a shrewd antique broker got most of it."

Big Catch

My first fishing experience was really a memorable one. One afternoon in late September, I walked into Jimmy's Bait and Tackle shop. "Hi, I would like to start fishing, but I never fished before and I have no idea how to start. Can you rig up fishing gear for me? It shouldn't be too expensive, since I might quit after the first trial," I said

"What do you like to fish?" the man behind the counter asked.

"Fish, any fish,"

"I meant fresh water or salt water?"

"Oh! Fresh water, because there is a creek behind my house."

"Do you want to use live bait or artificial?

"Artificial. I don't want to deal with slimy bait.

He selected a rod and several other items from his display racks and disappeared into the back of the store. Shortly after, he reappeared. "Here you are. With this lure, you can catch any fish, small or big. The line is twenty-pound tested, so you will have no problem fishing as big as 100 pounders with this rig," he said.

The lure at the end of the line surprised me. It was a seven-inch long realistic plastic fish which was equipped with six sharp, barbed fishing hooks.

"Cast this lure at the place where fish gather. If you cannot get any bites within ten minutes or after a dozen casts, change your location. Even the best fisherman cannot catch any fish if fish is not there. Good luck," he said.

Because of his comments, I had to revise my idea of fishing. I thought fishing was a waiting game and I would be happy if I could catch a couple of small fish after a whole day of fishing. I headed to the creek behind my house. My neighbor, David saw me with a fishing rod. "I didn't know you were a fisherman?" he said.

"Yes, a brand new one. I am ready to test my fishing skill for the first time in my life," I answered.

"You will have no problem catching a few. Even my grandson caught a dozen fish. You know the guy three houses down there? He caught a ten-pound bass here and has it mounted and hung in his living room."

"Ok, if I catch anything bigger than five pound I'll share it with you for tonight's supper," I said.

I had trouble casting the lure in the beginning. The first cast ended up too short and the lure tangled with grasses on shore. The second cast went to the middle of the creek but the lines entangled. I was aiming at the edge of the flat weed-bed near the other side of creek where I had seen herons catching fish. After several tries, my cast was successful and the lure dropped near the weed-bed. I felt a tug. I reeled in the line and caught my first fish, an eight-inch bigmouth bass. I thought, "Hey, fishing in Florida is easy. No experience needed. My first successful cast got a fish. No wonder people have to change location if they can't catch within ten minutes."

With several casts I got a total of three fish, all of similar size. I became more skilled in casting. So I aimed at another spot where I saw bigger fish jumping around. It was under overhanging bushes. I knew it was a difficult cast, but I had to try it to catch bigger fish. I cast carefully but the lure flew high and caught in branches. I tried to reel in the line, but couldn't. I loosened and retightened the line, but I couldn't free the lure from the branches. I tried all kinds of tricks, but I couldn't retrieve the line. When I pulled the line, the branches bent and never released the lure. Since the lure had six hooks, it was impossible to loosen them all. When one hook loosened, another one caught a different branch. I wish I had used a weaker leader, and then a hard pull would have broken the line at the leader. But the line had no leader and was all twenty-pound strong line. I thought of cutting the line at the rod end, but then the resulting line would hang loose in the creek and might endanger wild birds and turtles. My only choice was to pull hard and break branches. I wrapped my hand with a towel and pulled the line by hand. I pulled, one, two, and three. I was bouncing back and forth to shake branches. I made each pull stronger and stronger. Suddenly something hit me in my right thigh. It was the seven-inch shiny fish, "I got it," I yelled.

David heard my scream, "Did you get a big one?"

"Yes, a very big one. I need your help. Bring pliers, I can't remove the hooks."

"Ok, I will be there. How big is it?" David said.

Despite the pain, I had to say, "About 135 pounds."

Gimmee, Roseanne, Your Honor.

Pretending to fix my shoe, I carefully listened to the conversation of an odd couple at the next stall.

"Do you come here often?" a pretty young lady asked.

"No, I usually go to Monterey Street," the handsome one-armed man said.

"Do you play golf?"

"No, I just hit balls."

I was disappointed to see she walked away without further conversation.

It happened at Green Meadow Golf Center. I had been coming to this place almost fourteen months every day, as weather permitted, to practice my swing, trying to reach the 150-yard mark with my driver. This range was always crowded. One day I had to wait about a half hour for an empty stall, and then got a stall between the one-armed man and a kid of about ten years old. I immediately noticed the man was consistently hitting more than 250 yards with his left arm. The kid on my right was hitting 150 yards easily. At first, they intimidated me, but they also encouraged me. I would eventually be able to hit at least 150 yards, since a ten-year-old kid and a one-armed man could do it. All I needed was more practice.

After my retirement I decided to pick up golf for exercise, even though I never played before. I learned the fundamentals of grip and swing in an Adult Education Course. The instructor said that all I needed was lots of practice and occasional play on real courses.

After more than one year of practice and occasional play, I realized that the game of golf was more than putting a ball into the cup with a minimum number of strokes. The game of golf has lots of hidden traps for newcomers to the game. Golf is supposed to be a social game, but it was not social for outsiders or newcomers, especially a foreign-born beginner like me who has to face the double challenge of different language and culture, in addition to learning the rules of golf itself. For instance, some courses have a dress code of no T-shirt, no jeans, but they allow gaudy Hawaiian shirts and Bermuda shorts. As a novice to the game, I never knew of such a code until I got there and saw these rules posted in small print in a corner of the pro-shop. Rules of etiquette were worse. Nobody told me what they were. It appeared to me that somehow most experienced golfers scorned and were not willing to help ignorant slow-witted beginners.

On one occasion I played golf at a real 18-hole course. I intended to play alone, but the starter paired me with a stranger. Based on my limited experience, the biggest problem in a golf game was finding a ball after it was hit. When we had practiced on the outdoor course during our class, we stood together to watch where the ball would go when our classmate hit it. I found the best chance to see where a ball went was to stand far behind the line of shot to observe the direction of ball flight. So I did exactly the same thing during the game to be helpful to the stranger. When he was ready to hit his first ball, I stood way back from him, but on the line of his shot. He swung his club. Then to my surprise, the club left his hands and flew toward me. It almost hit me.

"Sorry, buddy, you mustn't stand there," he said.

Later I learned that standing on the line of shot was a violation of an unwritten rule of etiquette. Many golfers hate an observer standing on the line of their shot. The flying club was probably not accidental, but intentional.

After almost fifty years of residence in the U.S., I still have trouble understanding English, especially slang. In the case of golf slang, it was almost impossible for me to comprehend. I had no easy way to find out what "Liz Taylor", "Bo Derek" and "Frosty" meant. For any seasoned golfers, jargon and slang may be trivial, but they gave me embarrassment and headache. For instance, I was confused completely when I heard the following words, "Gimmee", "Roseanne", "Your honor."

I agree golf is a difficult game and very deep. It takes ages to master the game. I still go to a practice range to perfect my swing as often as my time allows. Someday I hope to master the game of golf, but I might not have enough years left to accomplish the goal.

Only a few days ago, we had a new neighbor who rented a house across the street. He was reportedly an avid golfer, but he had trouble finding a golf mate, since he was a newcomer to the community.

"Yashi, what is your handicap?"

"Left hip", I said.

"No, no golf handicap. I heard you play golf, don't you?"

"No, I just hit balls. A game of golf is too difficult for me. By the way, how can I figure out my golf handicap?"

I was disappointed to see he walked away without answering my question.

Space Travel

" **A** ttention, please. Flight 48 to Mars is boarding now." That was the opening sentence in my first book, titled "Space Engineering." I had dreamed of space travel since reading H. G. Wells' "Travel to the Moon." Soon after signing the Allies' Peace Treaty in 1952, Japan had reactivated research and development in air travel. We wanted to skip over air travel and formed the Japan Interplanetary Travel Association. Its senior member, Professor Endo, immediately started basic research on solid fuel rockets for future low cost passenger carriers. In the beginning we experimented with small "pencil rockets" to gather engineering data. Eventually, we succeeded in sending a baseball-bat-size rocket to a height of ten thousand feet.

Then came Sputnik. It changed everything. We got international attention. Someone broke into Professor Endo's car and stole important data. He was forced to abandon research because of minor accounting irregularities in our research fund. We disbanded the association and I left for the United States in pursuit of my dream.

I studied Astronautics at MIT, got a job in the space industry, and launched a satellite after five years developing it. Nevertheless, the dream of space travel eluded me. I applied for the scientist-astronaut position to NASA, but withdrew the application because of my accident. When I left that job, I formed a company to promote private space travel. I filed bankruptcy in 1970, due to funding difficulty. It was my last active attempt at space travel.

Ever since, I had hoped that some company would start commercial space flights. The possibility came in December 1990. A Japanese reporter, Toyohiro Akiyama, took a three-day trip to the space station Mir after paying three million dollars to the Russian space agency. Three million dollars was a lot of money and I couldn't raise that kind of money unless I won a lottery. But the situation changed again. An American billionaire, Dennis Tito, raised the price of Russian space travel to twenty million dollars. Even NASA changed its mind and planned to accept commercial travelers in the near future. The estimated cost of NASA travel was five to ten million dollars. The feasibility of commercial space travel was not my concern any more, but its cost was.

I still didn't give up the hope of space travel. Several commercial companies such as the United States, Russia, China, and Japan, were eagerly developing commercial vehicles for affordable space travel.

One morning, I received a phone call from Japan. It was Doctor Higashi, my old friend from the Interplanetary Travel Association. He had continued his research in Japan after my departure, developed the H-4 solid fuel rocket and launched the first Japanese satellite. He started a company called Explorer Travel to develop a low cost space travel system. According to him, the company had successfully developed a four-stage solid fuel rocket, a combination of Japanese and Russian technologies.

"Congratulations! You did it!" I said to him. "If I remember correctly, a four-stage rocket is riskier than the conventional two-stage one. How much of a risk factor is it, man's grade?" Man's grade meant that the chance of a failure would be one in one hundred or less.

"Unfortunately, no. Its chance of failure is one in ten, the same as the unmanned grade. We couldn't improve it because the Russians didn't allow us a flight test," he replied.

"How can you call it a space travel system? NASA will not send even a dog with such a system."

"That's one of the reasons for this call. I need your help."

"Name it, I will do anything to help you. We are old buddies," I encouraged him.

"I want you to be one of the paying passengers in the inaugural flight," he mumbled.

I gasped. I expected he would ask for my technical skill. I trapped myself with a big promise. "Sure, when will it happen?"

"Twelve months from today. Our funding will dry up unless we make the inaugural flight as scheduled. Once we make a successful flight, investors will flock around us."

"You said a paying passenger. How much will it cost?" I inquired.

"Three hundred thousand dollars. Sorry, our principal investor insists that passengers must pay their own fares. I thought that you would try this adventure and could afford the fare. If it is too much for you, say no," he pleaded.

"No, it's no problem. Actually, it is a bargain," my bruised ego quickly answered back.

My dream was much closer than I expected, but the price still seemed exorbitant. Should I take a ride in the half-cooked rocket to realize my life-long dream or not? My answer was definitely yes, but what would my wife think? I decided not tell her the risk part. When I told her about my adventure, she became enthusiastic at first.

Then, she murmured, "How do we get the money?"

"I can sell all my assets, including this house," I said.

"How can we live with no income, no house and no assets?" she questioned.

My inflated hopes shrunk. Our conversation changed to an argument. I had to concede that we couldn't afford the expense. Should I abandon my life-long dream? No, no way. If I abandoned my dream, then I would lose the meaning of my life.

I thought about the money problem and the risk constantly. I expressed my feeling and mental struggle in my journal every day. I wrote, "Remember I was one of the most creative managers. I have to find a solution." This journal writing helped me, but a solution didn't come easily.

Then, lightning hit me. "Bingo! I found a solution! This is it! The solution is to …"

"Honey, it's time to wake up. You will be late for your appointment," my wife said.

"What time is it?" I asked.

"Almost nine. Also you should look at this," she pointed at the front page of the New York Times.

Its headline said, "Scandal in Japanese Space Travel Business: One Scientist Commits Suicide and Others Arrested." According to the article, the prominent Japanese space scientist Dr. Masao Higashi committed suicide over a failed space travel venture, called Explorer Travel. Tokyo police arrested Prof. Tokuya Endo, who was often called Japan's Goddard, and five others for fraud charges related to the business.

My dream of space travel went back again to its permanent home: dreamland.

How to Catch Men

Several men surround Geraldine, despite her middle age, plain appearance and stooped, short stature. Geraldine is the focus of envious gossips among her contemporaries. Many single women in her community despise Geraldine's relationships, but secretly wonder how she can accomplish such impossible feats. These women think they are more attractive than Geraldine and many would agree with them. Nevertheless, they hardly have a chance to become acquainted with even one male. friend.

Geraldine's long time live-in boy friend died last year. She still lives in his condo, located in an affluent gated retirement community near the seashore. Geraldine is full of vitality, despite her knee surgery and other physical ailments. She does not play sports, but is actively involved in many community activities. She is the president of the singles group, of which more than ninety percent of the members are female.

One of the female members asked her, "How many boyfriends do you have now?"

"Let me see, Bill, Charlie, Dave, Tom; a total of four. They are not my boyfriends, just friends."

"Could you share with me your secret of attracting men?"

Geraldine replied, "Before answering your question, I will ask you a question. How eagerly do you want to attract men?"

"Very eagerly."

"How many hours do you spend every day thinking about how to attract men?"

"Well, a few hours every week."

"I am thinking how to attract men in every minute of my waking hours and during my sleep. That is the secret. Sometimes I fail, but I succeed often enough to accumulate my assets. If you want to make lots of men friends, change your priorities. Place man-catching at the top of your list."

Geraldine shows her belief in her action. For instance, when she plans a single's party, she invites men from a nearby marina. According to her, this assures that only eligible rich men will come, since boat-owners cannot be poor.

Geraldine is a skilled cook, but she prefers to eat out at well-known restaurants with a male companion. She often says, "I like good food, good booze and good companions, especially men who pay my check."

Geraldine is a sharp-tongued, sarcastic, witty conversationalist, but her trademark is her almond-size diamond ring. The glitter seems to hide all her flaws. She watches her pennies, despite her apparent wealth. She suggests to her companions that they go for an early dinner to take advantage of the early bird special, even though she never picks up a tab. In a restaurant, she consumes lots of drinks but she eats hardly any food. However, she orders a large meal, which ends up in a doggie bag.

When she becomes drunk, she boasts of her wealth. On one occasion a lady friend said,

"When I went to the Prince's State dinner, I had to rent a mink stole for one night."

"Mink stole!" Geraldine interrupted her. "I have three of them. I would have given one to you, if I had known that."

Geraldine lives alone in her condo, but she offers a room in her place to men, if the man meets her standards. Some bachelor boat-owners prefer to have land-based temporary living quarters while docked at the marina. Since many boat-owners cruise around a fixed route, they periodically visit the marina near her town. So she always has a male guest in her condo, sometimes more than one.

She shows her female weakness to her male guest, "Charlie, do you know anything about a computer?"

"Oh, sure. What's the problem with your computer?

"I cannot print the last two pages of a three-page document. Can you fix that?"

"Sure, simple."

When she leads him to her computer, he is surprised to discover that the document is her portfolio report from the Merrill Lynch web site. He suppresses his delight in figuring out her true wealth. The web page indicates that the document contains a total of three pages, but only the first page is displayed. He wants to see the last page, which would include the total market value of her portfolio. His repeated attempts fail to scroll the screen to see the last two pages. He struggles with the printer setting and browser parameters in vain. He gives up trying to see or to print the last two pages. His quick mental arithmetic indicates that from the first page alone the market value exceeds a million dollars.

"Well, this is a web report from Merrill Lynch. Something is wrong in their web design. We should be able to print any web page easily. So this is Merrill's problem, not your computer or printer. They should be able to fix it."

"Yeah, it has happened before, too. At that time, Merrill sent a technician to fix it. I'm sorry to bother you. I will call them tomorrow. "

"No problem. I am glad to help you any time," Charlie could barely conceal his excitement at his finding.

Note: I heard an interesting story from one of my computer club friends, who does freelance web page design. He told me he had a client who wanted to design a simulated portfolio page from well-known brokerage house. The request itself was unusual, but the most unusual part of the request was to make sure that the last two pages of the supposedly three-page portfolio would not be displayed or printed. Naturally, he couldn't disclose his client's identity, but he was intrigued by this unusual request.

Lucky Breaks

"Stop the test!" the nurse monitoring Mike's EKG screamed. The tread-mill slowed down and stopped. An aide guided Mike to a seat. He was out of breath. His gasps for air kept him breathing through his open mouth like a goldfish. Despite his condition, he didn't want to stop the test. He was supposed to work out until his heart rate reached 127 or he started having chest pain. He felt his chest pain but his heart rate was only 101, so he wanted to continue the test.

"Do you have chest pain or pressure?" the nurse asked. Mike nodded and pointed to his entire chest area, because he couldn't speak.

"Open your mouth," the nurse ordered and sprayed something into it. He was still gasping for air.

"Do you still have chest pain?" she asked. He nodded again. She sprayed again and said, "This is nitroglycerin to stop the chest pain."

A few minutes late she repeated the spray but Mike's pain didn't go away. The process was repeated once more without beneficial result. Eventually Mike could speak, "What happened to the test? I want to finish the test."

"It's off, canceled. You may be having a heart attack, since you still have chest pain after three sprays. We are sending you to the hospital. I already called the ambulance."

When Mike was finally settled into a bed in the Intensive Care Unit in the hospital, it was the middle of the evening. The doctors decided they would perform a cardiac catheterization the following morning to get an accurate image of the blocked heart arteries. It meant no food for Mike for the rest of the night, even though he had already skipped three meals.

The result of the catheterization was dramatic. He needed emergency bypass surgery because he had seven large arterial blockages. Unfortunately for him, the hospital was not licensed to perform this type of surgery. He had to be transferred to another hospital fifty miles away.

By the time Mike was settled in the new hospital it was nine o'clock at night. His first concern was food since he had not eaten for the past two days. The bypass operation was planned for the next day. That meant no food after midnight for him. He had only a three-hour window for his possible last meal. A nurse put together a food tray somehow, containing salad without dressing and turkey dinner without gravy. The heart surgeon who would perform Mike's bypass visited him. The surgeon said that he reviewed video images from the catheterization and he could do the bypass operation, even though there were so many blockages. Mike asked about his main concern: brain and neurological damage during the operation due to side effects of the heart-lung machine. Mike didn't want the operation to be a success with him ending up a zombie. He much preferred to drop dead of a heart attack than live with a semi-functioning brain. The surgeon assured him that open heart surgery was no worse than any other major surgery.

It was already past midnight when Mike finally fell asleep and an aide woke him up for another test. He transported Mike on a rolling gurney to another part of hospital. The long corridors were deserted and not many people were around. It was cold. He knew hospitals usually kept temperatures down to reduce chances of infection, but the desolate surroundings made him feel colder than usual. When Mike arrived at the Imaging Lab area, he was shivering and had to request extra blankets, not readily available in that area. He was surprised to see a technician still working at that hour. The imaging room seemed extra cold and dark, but Mike had to strip the upper half of his body for the test, ultrasound imaging on his neck area.

Next morning Mike was ready for the bypass surgery, but a nurse informed him that the operation was canceled. She also brought the good news that a blood test indicated Mike had not had a heart attack. Apparently the stress test was stopped just in the nick of time. Then a doctor came and explained that both of his carotid arteries had severe blockages, one 95% and the other 65%. The chance of having a stroke during bypass surgery was probably 80%. So they had to fix the carotid before the heart surgery. Then Mike remembered that he used to feel faint whenever he looked up. It had to be caused by the blocked carotid arteries. He had informed his cardiologists, two in the past five years, neither of whom paid much attention. So Mike was on the verge of having a stroke, too.

Those doctors hadn't done their job right. Mike felt his rage against them rising in his body, but he tried hard to control himself. He had to be careful not increase his stress level. He was lying in bed all the time, so he had no problem with physical stress, but he was prone to be affected by mental stress. He had to be doubly careful not to get angry or excited.

While he was thinking about that, a technician came in for another blood sample. Mike said, "Another man just left with my blood sample."

She said, "I got an order to draw your blood. The other man did his job and I have to do my job."

"Can't you coordinate this blood taking? Every time you people come my arms have to bear extra holes. Just today alone I have already been poked seven times for blood." Mike was really upset.

Gloria, his wife who was visiting at the time, intervened, "Mike, calm down. Don't jeopardize your good luck. So far you are lucky. You collapsed in the doctor's office, instead of the middle of nowhere. So you got the best available care in time. Now they discovered your carotid blockage before you had a stroke. This technician is just trying to do her job. When you get upset and have a heart attack or a stroke, then your luck will have run out. Remember you are still in the danger zone. Let her do her job; an extra hole in your arm won't kill you."

Mike was really lucky. He was again saved, this time by a cool-headed wife.

Did You Pay Your Electric Bill?

Gloria was relaxing on the porch, enjoying the soft breeze of South Florida winter. The telephone interrupted her.

"This is Mary, your daughter-in-law," the caller said.

"How was the cruise?" Gloria asked.

Mary didn't answer the question, but said, "Your son, Bob, is in jail."

"What happened? Did he bring pot back with him?"

"Not that. It was a simple misunderstanding, but we need $2000 cash to bail him out."

They had finished their Caribbean cruise pleasantly. They arrived at Miami on Saturday of Memorial Day weekend. As they went through the immigration check, Bob was arrested on the spot based on computer information. There was an outstanding warrant for Bob on charges of grand theft and being a fugitive from justice! Electro-Florida Company had made these charges.

Bob remembered an incident five years ago when he moved from Florida to New York City. Somehow payment of his electric bill was messed up and he owed $300. Not knowing the problem, he moved to New York, automatically becoming a fugitive from justice. Six months later Electro-Florida pressed charges against Bob and the sheriff's department issued an arrest warrant. When Bob moved back to St. Augustine, Florida, two years later, he found out about the warrant. He and Electro-Florida settled the issue peacefully, the company dropped the charges, and the warrant was cancelled.

Unfortunately, the warrant database in the Dade County Sheriff's Department didn't purge it, so the cancelled warrant was still listed as valid.

Bob had thought that might happen, so he was carrying the official cancellation paper, which included a telephone number for authentication. When the officer called the number, a recorded voice replied that the office was closed, and to call back within normal business hours, nine to five every weekday. They locked Bob in a holding cell.

When Mary was told that his bail was $2000, she thought it was a simple matter of posting a bail bond. Then she hit a dead end. Unluckily it was a holiday weekend and none of the bail bondsmen's offices were open. She found out that the police would not take personal checks or credit cards. The payment had to be bail bond or cash. So she needed $2000 cash and called Gloria for help.

Hearing Mary's story, Gloria couldn't help remembering her late father saying, "Pay electric bills even if you don't have money for food. Their collectors are worse than tax men and follow you even to Hell." Naturally she didn't pay attention. Who would imagine the company seeking an arrest warrant for a mere $300 payment? This was no time for recollection, but for action. She had to secure $2000 cash somehow. Her husband was still recuperating from a recent operation and not of much help. She didn't have that much cash lying around the house. To borrow the money, she tried to find an open bank, but found none. Employees of every bank in the region seemed to be enjoying the holiday weekend like everyone else.

The next idea was ATM machines. She used both her credit cards and obtained $1000 by using them up to their limits. She still needed an additional thousand dollars. She was reluctant to use her last resource, but told herself that she had to do it for the sake of her son. She was afraid of going to the sleazy part of town even in the daytime, but already it was dark outside. She drove to the store with a big sign saying "Checks Cashed" and parked as close as possible to door. Carrying the remote control of her car, and ready to press its alarm button. She entered the store, which looked like a jail house with its all windows and doors covered with iron grilles. Inside, there was barely enough room for two people to stand. This space was also surrounded by iron grids and a small window with a tray-size writing table opened in the cage.

A surprisingly friendly looking middle-aged bald man appeared behind the window and said to her, "May I help you?"

"Can you cash a personal check?"

"Sure, that's our business. Do you have identification?"

"Yes, a driver's license and a couple of credit cards."

"We can give you cash for a personal check or credit card, either way."

"What's the difference?"

"Ten percent for personal check and 15% discount for credit card?"

"Only 15% interest for a credit card? That's reasonable."

"Lady, it is not interest, it is a discount and I subtract that amount from your loan. If you borrow $1000, then you get 1000 dollars minus the discount rate of fifteen percents, 150 dollars. You would get 850 dollars cash."

"That's ridiculous!"

"Lady, this is not a bank."

"I am sorry. I need 1000 dollars cash until Tuesday, when a bank is open."

"You have to take a loan of 1112 dollars for a personal check loan or 1177 dollars for a credit card loan."

"I will write a personal check."

"If your check bounces, the fee is 100% per week. The amount of your loan will double every week until you pay it off in cash. I remind you that we have means to collect our debts."

Gloria was exhausted by the transaction of signing several papers and receiving the cash of 1000 dollars. Before she left the store, she asked, "Is it safe to carry the cash around here?"

The guy smiled and said, "No, but we provide you a bodyguard service free of charge. Where is your car? "

"In front of the store."

"That's good, our guy will watch you until you get in your car and drive away safely. Don't stop under any circumstances until you get out of this area." Then he turned around and called to the back of the store, "Hey, Joe! Escort this lady."

She loathed her son for putting her in such a position, but she also thought about his position in the jail.

It took her five hours to drive to Miami and meet Mary. It was almost midnight. They went to the police station where Bob was supposed to be held. He was not there. He had been transferred to another jail. Nevertheless they successfully bailed him out before 4 A.M.

She finally learned the true meaning of her father's advice and hoped that her son also learned the same lesson from his own experience. She also wondered what kind of experience her father went through; were collectors for electric bills worse than loan sharks?

P.S. It took another six months and 5000 dollars lawyer's fees to clear her son's record and to receive return of the bail money. I hope you already paid your electric bill this month.

CPSIA information can be obtained at www.ICGtesting.com
Printed in the USA
LVOW070737081212

310694LV00004B/19/P